THE FINANCIAL HUSBAND

THE FINANCIAL HUSBAND

H K FINLEY

* * *

The Financial Husband is a work of fiction. Names, characters, incidents, and places are either the product of the author's imagination or are used fictitiously. Any resemblance to actual persons living or dead, events, or places is coincidental.

CONTENTS

Chapter 1

ANNA BLUE AND THE MAN IN DELPHI POND

The dream startled Anna Blue awake. She bolted up in bed, her pulse racing, her heart pounding. Yet as she tried to recall the dream, her thoughts became as dense as the fog that hovered over Delphi Pond. Without a moon, the night was black and close. She looked at the digital clock on the bookshelf: three in the morning. Going back to sleep was impossible. Anna tossed the quilt back, sat up, and stood on the heated wooden floor. It was real wood, not a floating floor with the wood pattern photographed on the surface. Her mother, Maria, never went for anything but the real deal and neither did her dad, Richard.

The sliding glass door was already ajar about eight inches. Anna opened it wide. Like her parents, she slept nude with the door slightly open once winter started, and it felt like it would start early in Little Rock this year. The late October air chilled her bare skin, but it felt good as she stepped out onto the second-floor deck, which was less than fifteen feet from the eastern bank of the pond.

She could barely see the ground through the fog, clouds on land. As her eyes accustomed to the dark, Anna heard the water moving, slapping against the bank, and wondered why. There was no wind. What caused the ripples? She slipped on her wetsuit and readied herself to stand-up paddle. Careful not to wake her parents, Anna tiptoed barefoot across the living room and left through the front door. She had repeatedly begged for a set of steps from her bedroom deck that would lead directly to the ground but her dad always refused. He said they would create an open portal to her room. Anyone could walk up and stand in front of her glass door and watch her sleep. When she woke up screaming one night because she thought a man was standing over her, she quit asking.

Anna turned right to take the cedar platforms that led to the yard. She shivered with the anticipation brought on by her zinging intuition. Something was on the pond, or maybe it was someone, and she wanted to know. Anna ducked into the storage shed and pulled out her Jimmy Lewis stand-up paddleboard and her custom graphite paddle measured to fit her five-foot-zero inch height. Anna, small but strong, and well-muscled, was an excellent water person. She'd won medals for her high-school team in distance swimming. The mile was her favorite and she had participated in the Annual Waikiki Roughwater, a two and a third mile ocean swim, that past Labor Day.

Anna tucked the ten-pound board under her arm, held the paddle in the other hand, and headed toward Delphi Pond. She could tell from the temperature of the water that her thin suit wouldn't be enough to keep her warm if she fell in, which she never did. On the waves in Maui, she fell often, but the pond was a piece of cake compared to the Pacific. Attaching the board's leash to her ankle, she paddled toward the dock at the end of the pond closest to Cantrell Road.

Anna was paddling on this early foggy morning because the call—the pull, the whatever it was—demanded she do, and her instincts told her to heed. The drive to solve the unexplained often got her into tight situations and sometimes real trouble. As she neared the pond's center, the fog seemed to lower itself until it clung to the water and soon she could barely see past the front of the fiberglass board's nose. Anna kept going. Her headlamp was useless: the light bounced back into her eyes. She turned it off. Having grown up on the pond, Anna knew every inch and let her knowledge of it guide her in the direction her instincts told her to go.

Anna saw what she thought was a buoy hanging in the water in a place it was not supposed to be. Out of the side of her right eye, she thought she saw shapes moving behind the cattails near the bank. Her eyes wouldn't have been drawn to that section of the pond if it had not been for the glow of a small fire she noticed through the vegetation that clustered there. The movement happened so quickly she heard herself gasp. In her mind, a vision of three witches dressed in black cloaks sprang up.

Anna knew it was Halloween and figured it was probably trick-or-treaters. But then she remembered October 31 was also celebrated in another, more sinister way. Her imagination developed a scenario of a coven performing a ritual on the bank on this Wiccan holy day, the pagan new year honoring the dead, Samhain. It was a day of cleansing and releasing. Anna wondered who the campfire belonged to as her eyes searched through the fog hoping to find the shapes again when her paddle struck an object in the water causing her to almost lose her balance.

Suddenly two flippers appeared on each side of what she thought was a ball wrapped in duct tape; they flapped in the air and slapped the water. Her first thought was an otter but they didn't inhabit the pond. Then she saw the eyes and realized she was looking into the face of a human bobbing like a cork.

"How did you get out here!" Despite Anna's startled tone, it wasn't a question but more of a demand.

Tape encased the head and face except for the eyes and the nose. The mouth was taped shut. The tape crossed over the cheek, traveled around the back of the head, across the opposite cheek and back over the mouth again and again.

Tape wrapped under the chin, up the side of the face, across the top of the head and back to the point of beginning several times. If the hands had not been taped, the person might have been able to unravel it. But the thoroughly wrapped hands were as useless for this action as a seal's flippers.

Anna quit paddling. A shiver almost as strong as a rigor passed through her body. She could not imagine the terror this individual was experiencing.

"Swim to the dock. It has a ladder. Get out of the water. You'll freeze." As the words left her lips she realized she'd wasted them. The person couldn't hear or swim.

Arms flapped in response to her presence but the body didn't move from its position.

Anna figured she was looking at a tall man because the water at this end of the pond was around six feet deep and his chin was out of the water. Since he didn't move, she guessed he was snagged on one of the rotting trees beneath the surface or maybe, the thought struck, he was attached to something like a concrete block. That caused her to wonder if he was involved in a crime against a drug cartel or some other type of crime organization. Now, she feared him more than she wanted to pull the tape off his mouth and hear what he had to say.

Anna felt for the cellphone she'd stuffed into her suit and removed it to call 911. She stayed out of his reach. If he looked as if he would drown, she would come closer and let him hold on to the end of the paddle with his flipper hands.

From her lifesaving courses, Anna knew a drowning man was a dangerous man and his strength came from the adrenaline coursing through his blood. If she got in the water with him, and tried to free him, he could grab her and hold on to her, use her as a safety device.

Then she sat down on the board with her legs straight out in front of her and kept an eye on him as she prepared to punch in the three numbers when he suddenly sank. She waited for him to bob back up, but he didn't. She paddled closer to where he had been. All of a sudden, her board heaved upward and she fell into the water. Her cell sank. Anna surfaced and pulled her board to her using the leash.

Unexpectedly, she was jerked underwater. Strong arms wrapped around her shoulders. Anna struggled, twisting her body and kicking. His hold on her was strong and heavy. She felt herself tire as her lungs begged for air.

Remembering her lifesaving courses, she quit struggling and tried to sink, hoping he would let go of her. She ground her teeth into his forearm close to his wrist and bit down until her jaws ached and she felt his hold on her relax. Bending her knee, she kicked backward toward what she hoped was his groin and pushed herself away. She surfaced and swam until she was far enough to feel safe. Trying to regain control of her breathing, she pulled her board to her. Her arms shook as she climbed on. She'd find her paddle later. It wouldn't sink.

"Well, goddamn. What the hell are you doing out here at this time of morning?"

Anna jerked her head in the direction of the voice. Ron Cole switched on a lantern. Its soft glow illuminated the face of her neighbor, a man she'd known her entire seventeen years, the protector of Delphi Pond.

"There's a man." She paused for breath. "He's standing in the pond. His head is covered in duct tape and so are his hands. I tried to call for help. I think he's a criminal or something." The words rushed out until Anna ran out of breath. Her body shook from the cold and the terror of being pulled under and held. "How—how did you know I was out here?"

"Hell, couldn't sleep. Saw a lamp glowing in the fog, moving across the water and figured it was you. Then it disappeared. I was right on you when you flipped the board."

"I didn't flip it. He did. He tried to use me as a float. He's right over there." Anna pointed.

"I know where he is. Saw him. Figured I'd better check on you."

"He's drowning. I think."

Rapid splashing got their attention. Ron paddled his camouflage colored canoe in the direction and Anna followed, lying on her board and paddling like a surfer. Ron grabbed the man by the collar of his shirt and pulled his body a few inches out of the water.

"What the hell!" Ron kept himself in excellent physical shape, and although he was in his forties, he was as strong as he'd been when he was in the military, special forces—yet he couldn't pull the man into the canoe.

"He's caught on something." Anna's teeth chattered.

"Fella, I don't know what you did to deserve this but I'm going to give you some breathing room." Ron reached into his vest, took out a knife, slid it under the tape, and ripped the tape away from his mouth. A sliver of blood bloomed on the man's cheeks where the knife sliced his skin.

"Help! Help! Help me!" And then the man let out a scream that surely woke up all the four families that lived around Delphi Pond.

Ron gave him a jerk. "Shut up! Hold still! I'm gonna hand you this life jacket and you're going to hold on to it. If you fight me, I'll knock you out!" Ron shoved it toward him and the man grabbed it as best he could and hugged it.

"Undo my hands! God! Undo them. Help me. I'm tied to something. I can't move my legs." His flippered arms flailed as the words came in starts and stops. "I'm having a heart attack. I can't breath. My chest hurts."

"Well, calm down then. All that hollerin' isn't going to help. Try to steady yourself. You're more than likely having a panic attack."

Ron reached into his vest and drew out his cell. Anna expected him to call the emergency operator and was surprised when he said, "Brass. Wake up and get your ass down here to Delphi. I've caught something you need to see."

Cole spoke in a low tone and Anna had to read his lips to know what he was saying.

"Warren Mitchell." He paused. "I can think of millions of reasons. Looks like he's anchored to something just deep enough to keep his head above water. Will need a diver, Zodiac, paramedic. You get the picture."

Cole whispered as if he were afraid of being overheard. His eyes stared toward the bank where Anna thought she'd seen moving figures. She read her name on his lips.

There was a long pause while Cole listened and then he said, "I'll take care of it."

Cole ended the conversation and looked at Anna before she had a chance to question him. In a low voice, he said, "Before you start interrogating me, listen and keep your voice down. I suspect there is a cable or rope wrapped around his ankles and it is tied to some kind of anchor. I'm thinking the guys who put him here used a small boat. He's too far from the dock for someone to have just pushed him in at this spot."

"How do you know?"

"Experience."

"Do you think this is kidnapping and attempted murder? Like by the Mob, or a drug cartel, or gangs, or a bookie—or maybe not a bookie. Don't they just shoot people who don't pay them? I just got through reading about, oh, sorry. Go on. Please."

"It's about torture. To get him here, he had to be kidnapped and if he stays in the pond long enough he will get tired and won't be able to hold his head up and he'll drown. Maybe it is about murder."

"You said a name, Warren Mitchell, is that him?"

"How could you hear me? Never mind. The lip-reading. Little Snoop fits you perfectly."

"Who is he?"

"Mitchell screwed many people around here out of millions. Some of them retired folks and widows."

"I guess we can add them to the list of suspects. How do you know him? Why are you whispering? Why do you keep looking over there?" She indicated the bank where the fire glowed.

"I didn't say I knew him, just who he is."

"Why call Brass?"

"Chain of command." Cole reached into the inside pocket of his hunting jacket and drew out a flask. He handed it to Anna. "Warm yourself up. You're going hypothermic." Cole took off his jacket and put it over her shoulders. Her hands shook so hard she couldn't open the cap.

"Here." Cole poured some amber liquid into the cap. "Throw it back. It'll help." He took a draw from the flask, then another, and let out a belch.

Between the whiskey and the jacket, Anna's body warmed a little but her teeth still chattered.

Mitchell called out, "What about me! I'm freezing. Bring that over here."

Ron grabbed Mitchell by his tie and got in his face. "Buddy. I've done all I'm going to do for you. Shut up before I tape your trap shut again. I don't want to hear a peep."

Cole's eyes turned toward the bank and Anna's followed. "What's over there?"

"Stay here, kid. Keep away from him. Don't make a sound. Get flat on that board." Ron turned off the lantern and turned on his headlamp, changed it to pulse, and put it around Mitchell's neck then paddled away.

Anna strained to see what he saw, or hear what he heard, but her senses were dull from the cold. All she could feel was the condensed water drops in air that could not hold any more moisture crawling up her nose as she breathed and blinding her as she tried to see. The fog didn't keep her ears from picking up rustling sounds in the direction Cole had gone.

Chapter 2

DETECTIVE BILL BRASS

"Wake up." Ron Cole had commanded; but Brass wasn't sleeping, not even close. He was working on the final edits for a detective series scheduled to debut the next fall. It was inspired by a case he'd worked earlier that year.

In the doing of the thing, the writing about the case, the work he named *The Worthy Cause,* Brass saw where he'd gone wrong during his investigation. The case centered on celebrity convict Sabbath Dyme, a convicted child killer whose plight drew national attention and spoke poorly of the Arkansas judicial system. After his release using the Alford Plea, Dyme's wife, Dawn Daniels, claimed he tried to kill her by pushing her off a second story deck into Delphi Pond. For Brass, the only good thing that came out of the investigation was it inspired him to write a script: it sold, and that added to his bank account.

Brass slipped on his jeans and searched for his hiking boots. He wasn't about to wear his full quill ostrich boots mucking around a pond. The call from Cole brought him back in time to this same little body of water that had involved him with Dyme, Daniels, and Anna Blue. Brass already knew Ron Cole from the shooting range but the case had brought him into even closer contact with the ex–special forces man who had received his gravest wound as a civilian: a head injury that left him more aggressive than he'd been when in the service.

More than fifty years ago, the pond had been called Devil's Hollow, back when it was a swamp. Maybe today Devil's Pond might be a better name. It didn't seem to be a sanctuary in spite of the what the name Delphi implied.

Brass eased his six-four frame into his Porsche Boxster and called Police Chief Marshall Knight. "Sorry to wake you, Chief . . ." He told what he knew. They'd been roommates back in college and remained close friends. He wouldn't be in Little Rock now if it weren't for Marshall, and he liked Arkansas.

Brass also loved Wye Mountain and the home he had bought from the trust of Manny Walker. He'd never met Manny but felt he knew him since Brass had moved into the house with Manny's things still in place. He'd found a box with some of Manny's old clothes and from that learned they were the same height but Manny a little bit heavier. He kept the box and the discovery of it led him to buy the ostrich boots he usually wore. Manny had a pair of full quill: Brass would have worn them except they were a little too big, as were Manny's jeans. Also in that box, he found a bunch of old photographs of Manny and he kept those too.

Brass phoned his partner, Trudi Calasa, and told her to put a crew together based on Cole's assessment. He backed out of his detached garage and sped down his quarter of a mile long driveway to Highway 300 which would take him to Highway 10 and to Delphi Pond. The woods of Wye Mountain were forty-five minutes from the city limits of Little Rock. He took the curves of the two-lane fast and pushed the limits of his skill. He liked early morning driving, no slow-moving pickups or school buses ruining his ride.

At Wye Mountain, two hundred forty meters above sea level, the sky was black and clear with stars that looked like they were right on top of him. When he rounded the eastern shoulder of Wye, he saw the fog below and in the distance and knew once he got into it the going would be slow. No way he would get there before Trudi and the rest of the crew that would extract Warren Mitchell from the dark waters of Delphi.

Brass thought about Cole and wondered why he'd called him instead of the emergency operator. Brass mulled it over. Cole was a man who had a reason for every move he made. Already this case had similarities to the old Delphi case. Dyme and his wife were high profile in Arkansas and so was Warren Mitchell.

Mitchell, a fifty-five-year-old man accused of participating in a Ponzi scheme, had never been charged with the crime most people thought he committed. According to the Arkansas Securities Department, Mitchell was also a victim, which allowed him to continue to work as a financial advisor. Dyme's wife ran a non-profit con but was never caught, and Mitchell was a con of another stripe. Brass thought about the coincidence of two con artists landing in the same pond at night, plus Cole and Anna Blue being involved, and Brass himself called to sort it out.

Almost an hour after leaving Wye, Brass saw the misty image of flashing red and blue lights. He called Cole. Still no answer. He'd tried at least four times since leaving Wye and a bad feeling started creeping in his gut after the second unanswered call.

His cell chimed as he pulled off the road. "I see your lights. I'm walking toward you." Trudi Calasa didn't waste words with greetings or goodbyes and that didn't bother Brass. He liked brevity. Her habit of falling into pidgin took him some getting used to. Trudi, her mother Chinese and her father Portuguese, had been born in Maui. She graduated from high school there with straight A's and attended college in Boulder, Colorado, Brass's alma mater. She worked as a detective with the Denver Police Department before moving to Little Rock when her partner Greer took a job as a law professor at the University of Arkansas's Bowen Law School.

Brass's first concern was not Warren Mitchell or Ron Cole, but Anna Blue. The Blue kid was special, and he was fond of her. They'd talked occasionally over the past months after he'd put the Dyme case to rest even though it wasn't finished, in his mind anyway. Anna was fixated on finding the missing artwork that was part of the mystery and would run by him her findings and the theories that resulted. Now, according to Trudi's brief report on the situation, Ron and Anna had disappeared from Delphi.

"Did you call her parents?"

"We don't know if they are missing, as in missing persons. We just don't know where they are at the moment. There are no bodies floating in the pond, as much as we can tell considering the viz is about ten inches. I called for a dog. They cut Mitchell loose about ten minutes before you pulled up and he's on his way to St. Vincent's. Good thinking on the part of the guy who found him, putting that blinking light around his neck."

"Did our victim say anything?"

"Yeah. Said he was having a heart attack and then passed out. Had a bullet wound in his upper arm. From what I saw, it's not serious. We found the canoe; a graphite paddle, kind you use on a stand-up board, judging from the length it belongs to a kid; a man's hunting jacket; and the life vest the victim was holding."

"Anna Blue. She's short." Brass looked down at Trudi. From his vantage point, she was short too, maybe five foot four, and wide in a strong, muscular way. That there was any influence in her genetic makeup other than Chinese, he couldn't see. Her face round, her skin light brown, her hair black and straight. She wore it in a braid that ran down her back. Her eyes were deep brown and the shape of them told of her Asian ancestry. She wore what Brass called her uniform: khaki slacks and a Hawaiian print shirt.

Trudi was well educated. After earning her master's degree, she'd worked as a teacher, then a profiler, before settling into law enforcement. She carried herself with authority. Her English was impeccable, but when she chose to lapse into pidgin, her whole bearing changed into what he imagined was that of a sugarcane worker in the islands.

"Dog's here," Trudi said as she walked away.

Chapter 3

RON COLE AND
ANNA BLUE

While Brass drove down from Wye Mountain to Delphi, Anna used her arms to paddle her board toward the dock. She hung there, snugged up next to it, and took control of her thoughts, her breath, her shivering. Warren Mitchell was quiet and still. She wondered if he'd finally given up and let himself drown. It was in this period of stillness that Anna made the decision not to crawl up onto the dock and run home to get her parents but instead paddle to the shore where Cole headed.

The eastern side of the pond was congested in places with cattails, behind them a small clearing, and then the ground rose to meet the woods. A trail led through the old growth trees to a small shopping center on Cantrell Road, about a mile and a half from the pond. It was part of an old trail, wagon-train days old, that ran from Chenal Mountain to downtown Little Rock and beyond. Much of the trail had been destroyed by subdivisions, highways, and shopping centers but there were places it remained untouched.

Anna was glad for the fog. She felt protected by it. She paddled close to the water's edge and slid off her board at the place she thought she would find Cole.

As her feet found the bottom, a rough hand clapped around her mouth and she heard Ron Cole whisper, "Stay here. Stay low. I'll be right back."

Seconds later, Anna heard a gunshot and the sound of a splash as something big hit the water. Anna got back on her board and stayed flat.

Ron hit the water when he heard the shot and crawled back to where he'd left Anna. "I'm okay," he heard her whisper.

"Wait here. I'll check out the campsite." Anna didn't obey. She followed him. As they drew close to the cleared circular area where a small campfire burned, she heard Ron whisper. "What the hell?"

The cleared circle was completely outlined in hollowed-out turnips and miniature pumpkins. Each contained a tiny lit candle. Within the outer circle was an inner one lined with apples, gourds, black cats made of glass. On what looked like a ceremonial altar made of black stone lay nutmeg, mint, sage, oak leaves, nuts.

"Looks like an altar of sorts," Anna said. "Today is Samhain."

"Sam what?"

"The pagan new year, kind of like our Halloween, but not exactly. Do you think this has anything to do with Mitchell?"

"I don't know what any of this means." Cole's hand indicated the neatly laid out produce. "Looks like a magic show to me."

"Well, you know Halloween is all about honoring the dead, in theory anyway. Samhain is about cleansing and rebirth through death. Maybe they put Mitchell in the pond to, well, purify him or something."

"I'm not going down that crazy road. This looks like something a bunch of idiots who practice witchcraft put together. It took some strength to get

Mitchell tied up like that. No. These are unrelated. Look around. Looks like three women judging from the footprints."

Anna and Cole climbed the bank to where the woods began and tried to make up the distance between themselves and their prey, reaching the main trail where it ended behind a convenience store—only to find they were too late. They saw a white SUV speed out of the lot.

"Well, hell. Might as well walk down the highway. It will be quicker getting back to the pond. Brass is bound to be there with his crew."

"I'm going in to talk to the clerk," Anna said, walking toward the store.

"No, you're not. Leave it for Brass." Cole took her by the arm and nudged her toward the road. "We're outta here."

The cashier watched as a big man and a small girl walked out of the woods and disappeared into the fog.

While Cole and Anna were tracking the three women, Brass scrolled through his contacts and called Anna Blue's cell. It went straight to voicemail. He then placed the call he dreaded.

Maria Blue picked up on the third ring sounding like a person brought out of a deep sleep.

"Maria. Bill Brass here."

"What?"

"Bill Brass. I'm out here at Delphi. I need to see you and Richard. It can't wait."

"What's happened? Dawn Daniels dive back into the pond again?" Maria was awake now. Brass could hear it in her voice.

"I'll be at your place in a few minutes."

"Wait. Something is wrong." Maria sounded panicked.

"I need your help. I'm on my way." He hung up, not knowing what else to say. What was there to say? He knew nothing except that Anna disappeared into the fog with Ron Cole. That was scary and he didn't want to say it over the phone.

Brass walked along the west side of the pond across the dam road that ran under the second story deck of Connie Horton's pole house. He turned left and stepped on to the path that ran along the south end of the pond in front of Ron Cole's and Dr. Billy's houses and left again to the east bank where the Blues lived. He walked up the series of wooden decks that led from the pond to their house, just like he had done the first night he worked the Dyme case. Only this time, Anna Blue, aka Little Snoop, wasn't at home with her parents; she had disappeared. Maria and Richard met him at the door and the questions began before he crossed the threshold.

As usual, Maria did the talking and Richard the listening. "Anna's not in her room. What's happened? Tell me she's not hurt?" Brass saw the worry in her eyes and across her face.

Bill Brass told the little that he knew, and the Blues insisted they wouldn't sit at home and wait for answers. They walked with him back the way he had come. No one said a word.

Trudi met them on the dam road. "The dog found something, followed a scent along a path that led to a convenience store a couple of miles from here. It was going on the jacket we found."

"Who does it belong to?" Richard spoke for the first time since hearing the news.

"Sir, I can't say for sure. We think Cole. It was found near the area we found the canoe and paddle. It's all we had to go on. If you brought something of your daughter's, we will use it." Trudi stood with her legs a little apart, rooted to the ground, showing them through her posture the investigation was her territory.

"This is my partner, Detective Trudi Calasa. She's put this operation together. Trudi called for a tracker dog. Otherwise, we'd have to wait until some of the fog burns off to start the search."

"Excuse me." Trudi looked down at her phone and turned to walk toward Cantrell Road. It was a text from one of her men. Cole and Blue had been seen walking down the highway. She wanted to intercept them before they had a chance to speak with anyone. After a few minutes she texted Brass the news. No point torturing the parents.

Chapter 4

BILL BRASS AND ANNA BLUE

B rass waited until Cole, Anna, and her parents returned to their homes before he drove to the convenience store. He wanted to look at footage from
the security cameras, if they had any. To his surprise the pumps has non-ethanol
gas so he filled up his Boxster before going in.

The clerk, a young black man, or one of mixed ancestry, was studying a
biology textbook when Brass entered, showed his identification, and told what
he wanted.

The clerk ran his fingers through his thick, curly hair before he spoke, a
gesture of comfort. "The camera does not cover the far end of the lot, but I
can show you what I have. Although I do not think that will be necessary." His
speech pattern had a hint of something like a lilt and the timbre of his voice
told Brass that English wasn't the clerk's native language. "Besides, I know the
car. The lady buys her fuel from us. Like you, she uses the non-ethanol for her
Porsche. She has a Cayenne, a very nice car. She fills up two times a week."

"Do you know her?"

"Her name is Miz Katz. First name Brenda, I believe. Yes, Miz Brenda Katz."

"Was she with anyone?"

"She was with two other women. I have seen them before but do not know their names. Miz Katz is very friendly. She lives up at the top of the ridge in a beautiful house."

"How do you know that?"

"Oh, one time I went to her home to pick up toys and old clothes. We were collecting them down here for Women Helping Women and she asked me to come get them, which I was glad to do. So many boxes. Such a generous woman."

Brass thanked the clerk and left the station and drove to the ridge. There was a white Cayenne sitting in the circular driveway of a sprawling brick house. Two other cars were in the drive. He took down the plate numbers. He thought about knocking on the door but decided to wait until Trudi could go with him. He called the station and gave the numbers and then called Maria Blue and asked when he could see Anna. Maria told him to come over; they were so wired going back to sleep wasn't possible.

Anna was in her room when Brass arrived and Maria told him to go on in. After the Sabbath Dyme case, Anna occasionally called Brass to talk about "The Case." Anna, a natural detective, was determined to solve it since Brass hadn't. It wasn't really a case any longer, more a loose end in the Sabbath Dyme affair that wasn't worth the department's time to pursue. Brass lightly knocked on Anna's door, but she didn't answer. He heard music and the song surprised him. It was an old Toby Keith, or was it Willie Nelson, or both, "Beer for My Horses." He stood outside her door and listened to the lyrics, *"Grandpappy told my pappy back in my day, son, a man had to answer for the wicked he done. Take all the rope in Texas find a tall oak tree round up all them bad boys and hang them high in the tree, for all the people to see. That justice is the one thing you should always find . . ."*

Maria saw Brass standing at the door and moved past him, opened the door, walked in, and turned off the music. The room was Anna's bedroom and her office. The office part had been a bedroom for the baby that never came and then her mother had the wall torn down and Anna's room enlarged. She took up every inch of the space with her hobbies. Anna had her back to them, listing what she knew about the case on her board of possibilities. The sudden quiet startled her into turning around.

"Moma. Oh, Brass. Great." She smiled. "I've been wanting to talk about the man in the pond. Why does it still feel like night? I guess because it's dark. It was so exciting, all I've been able to think about."

"How about I bring in a couple of espressos and some calming tea to counteract it." Maria rolled her eyes and smiled. Tonight could have been a tragedy. They were lucky.

"I see it on your face, Brass. You're surprised I'm listening to country. Research of a sort. Dr. Baker, this retired professor from the university, gave a talk at my school about how the South is disappearing. About how TV and the internet have done what the Civil War didn't do, destroy the South and our unique culture. The South has a history of vigilante justice. I think that is what this whole case is about, so I put on these songs about retribution and . . . never mind."

Brass was glad to see she hadn't lost her ability to rattle on at length and provide information that actually informed.

"I haven't been around here too long," he said, "but long enough to know from personal experience there is a distinct difference between those born and raised here and those who moved from other parts." Brass walked toward the big white board. Possibilities were written in green and facts in red.

"Cole said something that made me think of that song. I got back to my room and downloaded it. It's all about getting even, answering for the wicked done, vengeance. I am thinking that is what Warren Mitchell being in the pond was all about."

"How do you know that was Warren Mitchell?"

"Cole recognized him. He told me about him. He said there were millions of motives, because of the millions of dollars he took from people around here and wasn't held accountable. I've been thinking about it. Ron saw three women on the bank, we saw their ceremonial site, and because last night was the Samhain, I believe they had something to do with him. Maybe they were clients, but maybe I'm not thinking broad enough. Ron was out on the pond. We didn't start out together, someone could accuse him of putting that guy in there, especially if they knew anything about his history. He is the kind of man Toby Keith sings about.

"I still think it was Ron who put Sabbath Dyme in that shed and gave him a few hard licks on the head. And I think he helped Dawn Daniels get the artwork out of Little Rock to where you couldn't find it. I can't prove that either, but I believe it. He is the vigilante type. Anchoring Mitchell in Delphi to torture him is something I could see Cole doing—especially if someone he cared about had been hurt by him. Can't you, Brass?"

Anna didn't wait for him to answer, just went on with another question. "Who were the women? I wanted to ask the night clerk at the station if he knew them or if they had surveillance tape but Ron wouldn't let me. He said to leave it to you. I bet the clerk knew at least one of them."

"Why do you think that?"

"The way I see it, they knew the trail was there, and that means they had been there before. That suggests to me that Delphi is in their home range. The store has gas, liquor, and food, and it stays open all night and has been there a long time. So it is possible, if the clerk has worked there awhile, he knows one of them. Maybe the one who owns the car buys gas there, and goes inside for gum or beer or something like that. Just a thought I had and could have followed it up if Ron hadn't of nixed the idea."

"You were thinking right. Brenda Katz owns the car. Why do you think Ron didn't check it out?"

"He's the kind who likes to make things happen not figure out why they did."

Maria walked in with espresso and her homemade biscotti. "Brenda Katz. I know her. She and her husband were clients of Jim Bud Haley's."

When Maria didn't elaborate, Anna reached for a biscotti to dip into her coffee and urged, "Go on, Moma. What do you know about her?"

Maria sat down and put her feet up on the ottoman. "I was Haley's consultant on jury selection and other things. Sometimes he would have me sit in when he talked to a new client, observe, pick up things, you know what I mean, watch their movements down to the smallest detail. That's where I met Brenda. First time I saw her, she came into the office wearing a mink coat and a big diamond ring, expensive clothes. Then she opened her mouth and her Southern drawl was so heavy it made her sound like an uneducated hick, except she wasn't. She graduated top of her class at the university. I thought she did this so people would underestimate her. When she dealt with her clients, or chose to, her diction was perfect, no accent."

Anna asked, "How do you know that?"

"Jim Bud Haley told me. I bet one of the women with her was his wife, Carol Ann. Brenda and Carol Ann are old friends and close. Really close. Carol Ann is in some ways like her. Their styles are over the top, fancy big houses, never see them without full makeup and in a stunning outfit, always smiling. Both are politically very astute and Carol Ann knows everyone."

Brass asked, "Did you know Carol Ann and Brenda outside of the work you did for Haley?"

Maria hesitated and focused on her coffee. "Professional women like myself were especially drawn to Carol Ann. Until I got to personally know her, I didn't understand it. Some women are strong in the workplace but abused by their husbands at home. I got a feeling she was one of them before she met Haley, but it was never confirmed. I know she converted part of her five-car garage into a studio apartment for women who needed to get away from their husbands."

"Moma, how do you know that?"

Maria wasn't sure she wanted to answer but she did anyway. She shrugged. They waited.

"I used to go to the Twenty-Eight Hundred Club, but that was more than fifteen years ago. From my work with Haley, I sort of knew Carol Ann but I'd never heard of The Club. That's what she called her house. Twenty-eight hundred is her address on Rodney Parham." Maria hesitated.

Anna and Brass waited. Each sensed Maria was trying to decide whether she wanted to go on.

"I was going through an emotional time trying to get pregnant again when I saw Brenda in the waiting room at the ob-gyn office, and we got to talking. I'd never been around her outside of her visits to Haley. She had five children so I told her my struggle to just have one more. It was late in the afternoon and she asked if I'd like to come with her to the Twenty-Eight Hundred Club.

"We just walked in, each of us carrying a bottle of wine, and there was Carol Ann sitting in the old rocker that she favored and women milling around drinking and talking. I was surprised when I realized I was in Jim Bud Haley's house.

"I went a few more times with Brenda and then started on my own. It was a safe place to talk and not worry what you said would come back at you. Sometimes men came but most of the time just women. Talking, listening, it was where I got the courage to refuse to keep on with the fertility treatments. I would probably have ovarian cancer by now from hormone injections, trying to have a kid that nature didn't want me to have, but my husband did."

Not much ever kept Anna Blue from having a comment but her mother's remark about nature and her husband did. She kept her mouth shut.

Brass was completely out of his element. All he could think of was how to get back on a subject that would move the investigation forward. He asked Anna to go over what she remembered.

Maria sat for a while and listened before she excused herself and let them get on to what they both loved, solving a problem. She walked to the kitchen and started rolling out more biscotti. Having her hands busy allowed her to examine why she went on the fertility rant. It really wasn't like her. She felt tears sting her eyes and let them flow. Her life would have been over if something had happened to Anna. That was what this emotion was all about, Maria told herself.

Anna dipped another cookie into her coffee. "You know, I think that bullet probably hit Mitchell. After I heard the shot, he didn't make a sound."

"It grazed part of his triceps."

"Do you think one of the women shot him?"

"Don't know yet."

"Ron said when he came out of the cattails, the women were already running from him. They saw him before he saw them. They had to go up the bank to get to the trail. When the gun fired, Ron hit the water and then he found me. If one of the women was aiming at Ron, she wouldn't have hit Mitchell unless she didn't know how to handle a gun. Or maybe, she wanted to hit Mitchell. Or maybe someone else was out there." Anna picked up her felt tip pen and made another notation on her board.

"I'll know more about that soon," Brass commented.

"I'm so keyed up; I've been reading articles, interviews with Arkansas people, and searching Stanford, Warren Mitchell, and affinity fraud. Do you know what that is?" She didn't wait for him to answer but kept right on. It reminded him of the Sabbath Dyme case and all of Anna's ideas and personal investigations on Dyme's wife.

"There were three seriously sick people that Mitchell cheated. All of them longtime clients of his. They weren't able to pay for their cancer medicines after their bank accounts were frozen by the receiver—the stuff that Medicare doesn't pay for, the extras that rich people can get and others can't afford. Their spouses claimed they died because of it. There was one woman who was in a facility for people with dementia and her husband couldn't afford to keep her there. He got sick taking care of her at home. It was too stressful. He had a heart attack and died in the house and no one knew for a few days. Days! Can you imagine that? He should have put her in hospice care. Insurance pays for that."

"You mentioned affinity fraud. How does Mitchell fit into that?"

"It's about stealing from people you have something in common with. Mitchell was big in his church. That was one of the places he mined for clients.

Wealthy people invested with Mitchell but so did others at his church, like librarians and teachers. He taught a Bible study class. They trusted him. Affinity fraud hurts more because the victim has a common bond with the thief. Sort of like your best friend steals your money. You've lost money and a friend. It hurts twice.

"Also he was a wide receiver for the Razorbacks and lots of his clients graduated from the U of A in Fayetteville and knew each other. He kept in close touch with them too. And it wasn't just rich people, he cheated. I read about one woman who came to Arkansas back in the days of the Cuban airlift. She worked as a maid her whole life and saved her money and she put all of it with Mitchell because the people she kept house for recommended him. She lost all of her savings and had to go back to work and she is in her sixties. He deserved to find himself in Delphi, if you ask me."

Brass wished he still had the energy and curiosity and drive that Anna Blue had. Being around her and her youthful enthusiasm for finding answers reminded him that he was sick and tired of squeezing answers out of people and running down leads that never panned out. He was still addicted to the hunt though and not ready to give it up, yet.

Chapter 5

THREE WIDOWS

B renda Katz lived on top of a ridge that overlooked the Arkansas River, a sub-division where professionals with new money had moved in the 1970s. She'd raised her five children there and now lived in the big house alone with a lot of company from grandchildren, as evidenced by the bicycles, tricycles, and other toys in her front yard.

Brass and Trudi knocked on Katz's front door at seven in the morning, and she looked to have been awake for a while judging from her appearance when she opened the heavy oak door.

Tall and slim, her dyed brown hair, streaked throughout with various shades of red, hung loose past her shoulders and was adorned with a beaded headband worn Indian style. This woman had seen a plastic surgeon more than once, Brass noticed. An exceptionally clear crystal hung around her neck on a leather cord. It seemed to guard her heart as it laid on her bare freckled skin in the middle of her chest. Brass wondered if Katz was going to a Halloween party. Dressed as she was, he could imagine her as a young woman smoking a joint at Woodstock. Her wrists, wrapped in bracelets of copper, silver, gold, and semi-precious stones, jangled when she moved her hands.

The detectives showed their credentials and asked if she would help them. Brenda Katz immediately asked if something had happened in the neighborhood. Brass said, "A man was found in Delphi Pond around three this morning. Your car was seen leaving the area around the same time. We want to talk to you about that. May we come in?"

Brenda didn't react at all to his words. The expression on her face didn't change, but maybe that was impossible considering the amount of cosmetic work. When she answered, the bracelets on her wrists moved along with her words. She signed as she spoke. "If it doesn't take too long. I am going to Grandparents Day at the school and I can't be late. Come in."

Trudi asked if she was deaf. "It's a habit," she explained, looking down at her hands. "My grandmother was deaf. I like to say my hands do my talkin'. I have to remind myself to keep them quiet." She laced her fingers together.

Although short on time, she gave them a leisurely tour around her house. She was proud of the river view and the name of the architect who'd designed her home. She showed photographs of her five children, all professionals, two doctors, two lawyers, and an accountant, and her thirteen grandchildren.

When Brass asked why she and her companions were out at that time of morning at Delphi Pond she said, "We were celebratin' Halloween, Wiccan style."

"What is that?" Trudi asked.

"You chant and eat, honor your ancestors, that sort of thing. It feels kind of like bein' in church except it's not a religious thing. Kind of hard to explain. There is this website called G-o-o-g-l-e where you can find all you want about it."

"Judging from your campsite, it looked like you all spent a great deal of time and effort on it. What time did you arrive last night?" Brass asked.

"I'd say we got to our spot a little before midnight."

"Why not park on Cantrell? There's an easement. You could have parked there and it would have been closer to your campsite."

She smiled, showing off straight white teeth. "It was not about gettin' there as quick as we could. It was about takin' time, embracin' the night. It was about the process of endin' the old and bringin' in the new. The walk through the woods helped set the mood.

"Are you plannin' to arrest us for tresspassin'?" Brenda paused and smiled. "When we were kids we played on Delphi all the time, got there by the trail. A church owns it now but the trail doesn't go anywhere near the church building."

Trudi paused, trying to get a better read on Katz. "Did you see lights or hear sounds, maybe a gunshot, coming from the pond?" Brenda said she did not hear a gunshot or see anything like a light coming from the direction of the pond.

Trudi's questions took on an incredulous tone. "Are you sure, ma'am?" She paused. "Did you see anyone in the woods around the pond?

Katz didn't respond.

"A man was tied up in the pond near your campsite. There was a blinking light around his neck. You were right there not fifty feet from where he was found. A shot was fired. You must have heard it."

"The fog rolled in after we got there and it seemed to close us off from the world."

Acting as if it just occurred to him, Brass asked, "Do you know Warren Mitchell?"

"Yes, I do. Why?"

Trudi thought Brenda would ask the obvious, *Was he the victim?* She said nothing though and waited for Brass to continue.

"Warren Mitchell was the victim. How do you know him?"

"I've been a client of his a long time. I'm sorry to hear that. Is he okay? What happened? I've known him for years." It was clear from her response, Katz was shocked.

Brenda Katz didn't appear to be holding back or lying but Trudi felt something was off.

Brass asked and she gave him the names and address of her two companions the night before, Isabelle Hart and Carol Ann Haley, the owners of the cars he had seen parked at her house earlier that morning. He would get around to another interview with Brenda Katz, give her a little time to think, and maybe something helpful would surface.

As soon as the detectives were out the door, Brenda went to her landline and called Carol Ann. "Two detectives were here. They know we were at the pond and wanted to know what we were doing there. They said Warren Mitchell was found in the pond last night. Can you believe that?"

Carol Ann asked, "Did you keep quiet about hearing a gunshot?"

And Brenda said she did. "You call Isabelle, Carol Ann, and tell her. I have to get going. I don't know if they are coming to your house or hers but they are on a mission."

While Brenda was alerting her friend, Brass and Trudi were turning right on Cantrell Road. They drove a few miles and turned onto Penal Farm Road.

The road once led to a prison farm where convicts were used as laborers in the fields but that was decades ago. The old farm had been bought by a developer and transformed into a small exclusive subdivision. The ten lots of four acres each ran along the bank of the Arkansas River.

The homes were located in the one-hundred-year floodplain but most were not elevated on piers. Growing up on Maui, Trudi had never seen houses the size of these until the island started developing and rich folks from the mainland began building houses ten times the square footage of the one she grew up in. These gluttonous Maui mansions were usually only occupied a few weeks out of the year, and she was prejudiced against them. The ten homes on the river were even bigger.

Unlike the other drives they passed, the house they were headed toward did not have a paved driveway. It was old style with brick pavers in the grass for the tires to pass over. Willows lined the sides of the architecturally inspired curved drive. Brass pulled up to a low stone and cypress fence. They walked through the open gate and toward a path that meandered through an oriental garden to an arched wooden bridge over a koi pond.

"Wow. This looks like a resort, Grand Wailea or Four Seasons," Trudi said.

A man stepped out on the path. He held a machete. The small Latino looked to be in his early sixties but it was hard to tell his age. He wore work boots, a long-sleeved denim shirt, baggy jeans, a floppy hat. In barely understandable English, he told them that Isabelle Hart would not be back until three that afternoon. After following them out of the garden, he shut and locked the gate.

When the detectives returned that afternoon, the gate was open. Brass and Trudi crossed over the bridge that spanned the koi pond. The steps to the house started on top of a big square, flat, rock in the center of the pond. A waterfall created from field-stones fell ten feet into the water where the big colorful fish hung out.

"Who puts steps in the middle of a pond? That spiral staircase isn't for the handicapped, that's for sure. Not even a handrail. Who would want to carry a load of groceries up these? Probably an elevator somewhere." Trudi talked to herself as they walked.

The elevated house owned by Isabelle Hart sat twenty feet from the bank of the river. As they climbed the steps, Brass noticed the water was running high and fast. There was no fancy landscaping on the river side of the house. Just the field and a few goats and a couple of horses keeping the grass down.

They reached the top and stepped onto the wide wooden deck that ran length of the house. A woman sat at a table at the far end. Her bare feet rested on the tabletop. Brass and Trudi walked toward her but she didn't get up, just waited for them to approach.

Isabelle Hart was a small woman in her sixties. She wore her gray hair cut short, no makeup, or jewelry. Her face was weathered but her skin looked soft and clear. Brass saw no signs of a face-lift, fillers, or Botox. Her green eyes were sharp and observant. She looked to weigh about a hundred ten pounds. She wore a tight long-sleeve top, a pair of fitted jeans, and no shoes. Although she had not moved from her original position, he could tell by the length of her legs she was probably five foot two. It would be easy to describe her as plain but she was not plain at all. "Essential" was the word that came to Brass's mind. He wondered if the interior of her home was as spare as its owner.

"Brenda told me a couple of detectives would probably stop by. She said you found Warren Mitchell in the pond last night." Isabelle Hart didn't waste time on small talk.

"I'm Detective Bill Brass and this is my partner, Detective Trudi Calasa. We'd like to talk about what you and your companions were doing at Delphi Pond early this morning."

"Have a seat." She gestured toward a couple of wicker chairs. "Would you like water? I have sparkling or mineral. No soft drinks."

Hart wasn't going to invite them into the house and that made Trudi want to get a look inside of it.

"Nothing for us," Brass said.

"Suit yourself. What do you want from me?" Her tone was exact but not unfriendly.

"Before we get started, may I use the restroom?" Trudi asked.

Isabelle indicated a door. "Right in there."

Trudi opened the frosted glass door to find herself in a large bathroom tiled in white from floor to ceiling. It contained a shower, a sink, a toilet, but no entrance to the rest of the house. She flushed the toilet without using it. Isabelle Hart was doing the questioning when Trudi returned.

"So, Detective Brass, tell me what Brenda told you. She has an excellent memory, great at bridge. If I can add anything, I will. That will be the most efficient."

Trudi spoke before Brass had a chance. "No, that is not an efficient way to discover what you saw or heard or remember. The best way is for us to ask the questions and you answer them."

"Is that right?" Hart tilted her head slightly to the right as she delivered the words with an extra lilt to her Southern accent.

Trudi took the lead and Brass observed.

"What time did you arrive at Delphi Pond?"

"I can't say for sure. We pulled into the gas station lot after eleven. We walked through the woods to get to the pond and I am not sure how long that took, maybe twenty minutes."

Brass watched Isabelle Hart as she answered questions. He looked for signs of nervousness, anything that would give him a clue if she was hiding anything or lying. Her story agreed with what Brenda Katz remembered. Both denied seeing or hearing anything unusual until a man dressed like a hunter came out of the pond and frightened them. It was Brass's guess that Mitchell had been soaking in the water less than two hours before Cole and Anna found him. That meant Mitchell was put there while the women were at their campsite. The only thing separating them from Mitchell was fifty feet of water and pond vegetation.

"Did you hear a gunshot?" Trudi asked.

"No."

"The man you describe as the hunter said someone from the direction of your site fired at him."

Since it wasn't a question, Hart didn't comment.

"Did anyone in your party carry a weapon that evening?"

"I don't own a gun, and I wasn't carrying one."

"What about your companions? We found a cartridge case near your campsite."

"I didn't see a gun." She hesitated. "I guess you don't understand why we were there. It was not a campsite but a ritual site. We wore ritual robes. There are no pockets in them. Underneath we were naked, no bras, no panties, no other garments. The only reason we wore shoes was the walk through the woods. We took them off when we got to the circle."

Brass tried to imagine three women in their sixties roaming the woods at night, naked under long robes, conducting some sort of Wiccan ceremony on the bank of a pond where a man was anchored up to his chin in the water, and they didn't see or hear anything. A gun was fired close to them and they didn't notice that either.

"There was quite a bit of work done on that site. The clearing was surrounded by rocks, candles, the hollowed out turnips, and so on. Did you bring those things with you last night?"

"No. We set up that afternoon."

"Was a gun brought in with those supplies?" Trudi's tone had an edge to it and Brass couldn't figure why unless it had something to do with her restroom visit. It wasn't like her to take over an interview after they had agreed he would have the lead.

"Detective Calasa, this was a cleansing and honoring ceremony. And, judging from the ancestry on your face, you should know something about honoring the dead and cleansing rituals. You don't enter into a ceremonial circle like you would a cocktail party or a shooting range." Hart's voice was flat. "I already said I didn't have or see a gun."

Brass saw Trudi bow up at the word "ancestry" and before her tongue went acid he interrupted. "Excuse me. Ma'am, what is the ceremony about and why did you need to conduct it at Delphi Pond?" Instinct told him this was the question he needed to ask to understand these women. Trudi had not provoked Brenda Katz nor had she been aggressive with her as she was being with Isabelle Hart and he didn't get why.

Isabelle was aware from her addiction to crime fiction that detectives liked to come back around to a subject from various angles, looking for inconsistencies and forgotten information. She wasn't impressed with either one of these but, having just finished a Google search on Brass, kept an open mind.

"Samhain," she said. "Is that what you are asking me to define? It means the end of summer and the beginning of winter. For many women, it is the beginning of the spiritual new year. We made our circle and performed our rituals to honor our dead and to cleanse and purify ourselves."

"To cleanse and purify yourselves?" Trudi asked. Brass didn't like the undertone in her voice. "Or were you cleansing and purifying Warren Mitchell in Delphi Pond? Did you and your friends put him there?"

If Trudi meant to fluster Isabelle Hart, she did not. So she pursued. "Warren Mitchell. How well do you know him?"

"Quite well. My late husband and I were his clients. After Dan was killed, he cheated me out of three million. I sued him. Got nowhere. I think that says it all."

"It says you have a strong motive to kidnap and torture him." Trudi's tone was abrasive and Brass didn't like it.

Isabelle shot back, "You're a drama queen. Not a healthy trait for a cop."

Brass wanted to get back on the topic of why she and her friends were at Delphi that night. He leaned toward her and asked, "Why Delphi? Was there a reason to have your ceremony there?"

"Since I did not have anything to do with Warren Mitchell being in the pond, I don't see a reason to give you my personal motivations for the rituals I choose to perform, where I perform them, or on what day, unless"—she looked at Brass—"you want to use me in one of your scripts."

"Humor the writer in me." Brass smiled as he said it.

"Let me think why I should make your job as a writer or a cop easier. Is it because you are wearing a custom-made belt buckle with the numbers four, twenty-three, forty engraved on the back?"

Brass instinctively touched the buckle.

"I believe you've gone a little white, Detective?" She grinned.

This woman reminded him of an older version of a witness in the Sabbath Dyme case, MB Bienville from New Orleans. He had to stop himself from making a tally of the similarities between the Dyme case and this one so he could fully engage in what was unfolding.

Hart turned her green eyes and her hard stare on Trudi. "I can see you are dying to get a look inside my home. That old 'I need to use the restroom' ploy didn't play out for you, did it? I could say go in and look around but I won't. I don't let strangers into my personal space, especially those who think I am a liar and a kidnapper. Your energy would contaminate my space. I would have to call in a shaman and have it purified. In fact, you might want to go for a personal session with one yourself. I think it could clear a few of your congested chakras."

"Enough." Brass stood. He let his voice relax before continuing. "Ma'am, I would like to interview you at the station. I see that you're a private person and would be more comfortable in a neutral environment. Tomorrow morning, I will be in at eight and would like to see you before nine. I hope that works for you."

Hart stood for the first time. "That works."

Isabelle escorted them out. She stood at the gate until they drove away, then pulled out her cell and called Carol Ann. "They're on their way to your place."

As soon as he put the car in gear, Brass turned to his partner. "What was that about!" It wasn't a question but a demand.

"Something's off about her. I smell it."

"That is not good enough. We agreed I would take the lead. You came back from your bathroom break and you were aggressive. I want to know why."

Trudi hesitated. "I go to toilet and shut the door. Suddenly, I get da chicken skin. I feel anger toward her and went with it."

"That doesn't make sense. Maybe we would have gotten more out of her if you'd stuck with the plan instead of going all chicken skin on me." He looked over at Trudi. Her eyes were on her smartphone.

"Hart knew what was on the back of your buckle. That should have given you plenty of da chicken skin. What was that about?"

Brass didn't reply.

They drove in silence the rest of the ten minutes it took to reach Carol Ann Haley's house.

After getting the heads-up from Isabelle, Carol Ann went to her bedroom to change and freshen her makeup. She had just been to the salon so her hair and nails were perfect. When the bell rang, her little dog, a Maltese-poodle mix, went crazy barking and jumping. Jazzy Marie knew the doorbell meant a stranger.

When friends came over, Jazzy didn't make a sound when they walked in without knocking. She escorted them back to the bar. That's what Carol Ann called her den, but it was more of a salon where friends stopped by after five for drinks and conversation. Even a few of her friends now in AA still kept the habit of stopping by. Conversation was the draw.

Carol Ann let the bell chime a couple of times before she picked up her dog and opened the door.

To Brass and Calasa, the two were a still life in white. A very curvy, older woman wore white slacks, a long-sleeved low cut white blouse, white and silver slippers. She held a little white, fluffy dog. Carol Ann's skin looked as if it had never seen the sun and the whiteness of it was set off by the blackness of her hair and the style. It was parted in the middle and blunt cut at chin level. Obviously, it was dyed but an excellent job. Her red glossed lips were tastefully plumped with filler and Botox relaxed the line between her arched brows. Her eyes were brown enough to appear black.

"Now come on in, ya'll. Isabelle said she had a visit from the police about Warren being in the pond and what we saw—or didn't see—and heard out there. It's all so exciting. Poor man, his life has gone down the drain lately and here is something else to worry him. I know your boss. Marshall and I are old friends."

Carol Ann chattered on as they followed behind her down the long hallway, the walls lined with a mixture of styles ranging from Oriental wood blocks to contemporary abstract paintings. "Marshall stops by here at The Club some-times. Oh, well, you can't be interested in that. Here we are," indicating a dark wood paneled room that looked out on her swimming pool. She offered them a choice of top shelf liquor, beer, wine, or sparkling water.

Brass and Calasa chose water and Carol Ann did the same, but she wanted a shot of bourbon, or two.

Carol Ann's version of events coincided with Brenda's and Isabelle's, not surprising either detective. Jazzy Marie warmed to Brass right away. When the dog jumped up in his lap, Brass let it sit there. Trudi asked if she could look at the artwork and Carol Ann encouraged her to enjoy her collection that lined the walls of her living room and hallway.

"Just look around all you like. I love it when guests appreciate my home. Holler if you have any questions."

Carol Ann said to Brass, "So you want to know why we were at Delphi instead of, say, the pool here at my house? Is that what you're wanting to know?"

"Yes, ma'am." Brass stroked the little dog. He'd thought about a dog, one that would roam around his place at Wye, a big one, a hound, maybe a Rhodesian ridgeback, when he'd first moved up there. Manny had a golden retriever but the neighbor took it when he died. Sometimes it came around and Brass fed it.

"I do know about that criminal pushing his wife into Delphi and you investigated it. And now here you are again. I would say Delphi is calling you. Maybe you should have a channeled reading about that." She waited for Brass to comment but he sat there and waited, petting Jazzy. Carol Ann liked that, the petting and the waiting for her to speak.

"Let's see. Well, me and Brenda and Isabelle have been going through a spell of what we call the troubles. It was Brenda's idea to go see Laurel Moon and we did. I don't know if you know her but anyone who needs to find a direction sees her. Some cops from Chicago called Laurel in on a case about a missing woman doctor last year. She even helped the police here several times. She is wonderful. So we got involved with her and I say it was the best thing ever, considering."

"Considering?"

"Well, I suppose Brenda told you our husbands died, suddenly died, about three years ago. Us, best friends since grade school, and our husbands all dead in the spring of the same year. I mean violent deaths, accidental of course, and here we are widows together. It was in the paper. Some reporter doing a human-interest thing called us. We wouldn't talk to him, but that didn't stop him from writing about us. I saved the article." She got up and went to a bookshelf, removed a lacquered box, and set it down on the table in front of them. "Here it is."

Brass scanned the article. "Please, if it isn't too painful, I'd like to hear you tell me."

"Well, Brenda's had a tree limb fall on him on a camping trip when they were floating down the Buffalo. I mean a storm came up and they made camp and the wind—there was a tornado in the area—and a big limb came down and hit him on the head. Brenda was alone and she dragged him into the canoe and paddled to get help and they hauled him off to the hospital. His brain was coming out of the crack in his skull but he was breathing and Brenda had to tell them to just do nothing. It was awful.

"And then, my Jim Bud augured his plane into the ground at North Little Rock's airfield. I was with him. Not in the plane when it went down. We landed there to get fuel. Then he told me to stay on the ground, said he thought he felt something funny when we landed, and wanted to check. I was watching him make the approach and next thing I knew he crashed.

"A few weeks later, Isabelle's Danny landed some kind of experimental plane in the top of a tree and when he released his seatbelt and tried to climb out, he fell and broke his neck. Isabelle stayed put in her seat and called 911 and eventually the Pine Bluff fire department came and rescued her. He died instantly, they said."

Brass was surprised at her presentation. There was no emotion in the recounting. He wondered if the woman was suffering post traumatic shock. "What does this have to do with your presence at Delphi last night?"

"It is about healing. We needed to heal, to understand, to accept, to move on. In what universe does this kind of thing happen to three friends, in a three-month period, where their husbands die right in front of them? We needed healing and acceptance of what happened."

"Why Delphi?"

"I can tell you aren't from around here, honey, so probably don't know about Delphi Pond. That old man Horton, the grandfather of that bitch Connie, took a sacred place and desecrated it for his own selfishness. He took the Hollow and destroyed it. He flooded it to make Delphi Pond. He tried to destroy the spirits that lived in the swamp, but he didn't. Uncle died in that pond. The Hollow took him because he didn't fight for it. That was his sin and his punishment. The submerged rotting trees trapped him and he drowned."

Brass was confused. "I thought it was a black preacher who drowned in the pond. You say it was your uncle?"

"I didn't say that. I said Uncle. That's how he was known. His wife worked for my grandmother, keeping house and helping raise us kids. My grandma lived on that ridge above the pond where that church is now. Her family owned property all the way to what is now the interstate for a long time. Sold it piece by piece until there were just a few acres left. I grew up there. My daddy died when I was young and we went to live with Old Grandmother. My mother worked. I was just a girl when the swamp was dammed up but it broke my grandma's heart, and my mother's, and the hearts of many who lived out the highway."

"What did Uncle have to do with it?"

"According to my mom, there was a big uproar about it and Uncle used his pulpit, his Sunday sermons, to calm everyone down until old Mr. Horton got the job done. Then Uncle started having baptisms there to show it was God's will or some such crap, and on and on. You get the picture, don't you?"

"And you are saying you and your friends decided to have your ceremony at Delphi, uh, why?"

"Because it is a spiritual place that is trying to heal itself. Like we are trying to heal ourselves. The Hollow wants free of the water but that won't happen unless someone comes in and blows up that dam Horton built, and that's not gonna happen, and if it did, the state or whatever would build it back. Don't you see, we identify with Delphi's troubles. I identify with it the most. I grew up on it back before Horton and those other people built houses around the pond. It wasn't bad enough Horton killed the Hollow, the others had to go and hem it in with their fancy houses."

"Why do you think Mitchell was put in this particular pond?"

"I don't know. It is easy to get to from the highway. I do think that man must have needed purification or punishment," Carol Ann said. "Now, I am going to have a bourbon because I've said all that I'm going to right now." She got up and took the Woodford Reserve off the shelf. "I am exhausted from all this talk."

As she was pouring her drink, Brass asked how she knew Warren Mitchell.

"He is my financial advisor. One of them anyway. I've known him for years and his wife, Judy. She has cancer."

"Isabelle Hart said he cheated her out of several million. Did you have any trouble with him?"

"Warren lost a couple of million of mine but he lost money too. Stanford fooled him. He is not a thief, just gullible. I've forgiven him and moved on."

"What about Brenda Katz? Has she forgiven him too?"

"She still does business with him like I do."

"Of the three of you, only Isabelle Hart quit using him and sued him?"

"That's right."

Trudi was standing in the door that led from the kitchen and bar area. "Ms. Haley, do you own a gun?"

"Yes, I do. I have a permit to carry. Want to see it?" Carol Ann got up and went into the kitchen for her purse, removed the small revolver, and handed it to Trudi. It didn't have anything to do with the cartridge casing found at the scene.

"Did you husband have a gun, perhaps?"

"Jim Bud had a whole room full of them. That collection in the living room belonged to his daddy and it passed to him."

"I mean ones that are not antiques," Trudi persisted.

"He had several, kept one next to the bed, one in his car, in his plane, a shotgun in the bedroom closet, and one at his office. Why are you asking?"

"A shot was heard around the time the victim was found. We found a cartridge casing at your campsite."

"Are you asking me if one of us shot him? The answer is no."

"I have to ask. Did you hear a shot?"

"No. We had on our headphones on. We were chanting. If someone shot a gun we couldn't have heard it. We were in a trance state. Maybe it was that hunter who came out of the pond."

"He said the shot came from your direction."

"If you look hard enough you will probably find hundreds of bullets and casings around there. When I was a kid I remember people used to go down there and use the snapping turtles for target practice. Maybe they still do."

"May I see the headphones?" Trudi asked. Neither Hart nor Katz had mentioned them.

Carol Ann brought her smartphone and the headset and handed them to Trudi. "These are the kind you use on the airplane so you can't hear anything except what you want to. They helped us get into a trance state."

Trudi put them on. The volume was high and the chanting made her head swim.

"Were all of you listening to the same thing with the same kind of equipment?"

"Of course."

"How did you happen to notice the hunter coming from the pond, if you were in a trance?"

"I didn't. It was Isabelle. I was all out there in space, at one with the universe and the dead, and suddenly the headset came off and she was telling us to run that a man was following us. It took a minute for me to comprehend what was happening."

"How did she see him if she was in a trance?"

"I was in a trance. I am supposing she was too. I don't know. Maybe she felt him. She is very sensitive to the energy of others. She won't let anyone in her house she doesn't know and some people she does. Says she doesn't want strange or toxic energy in her space. She can feel it. That started right after her husband died."

"Was it her idea to have the ceremony at Delphi?"

"No. It was our idea after we started seeing Laurel Moon, or maybe it was Laurel's. I don't remember. Delphi is spiritual."

"May I see your husband's guns?"

"I can go round them up but you said you found a cartridge casing. All of his are revolvers. If you want to look at them, I'll go get them."

Trudi did.

"I don't know what happened to the shotgun. I might have lent it out. I don't remember." Carol Ann laid the guns down on the coffee table, very carefully, since they were loaded.

"What about Ms. Hart and Ms. Katz? Are they gun owners too?"

"No."

Just when Trudi felt like she was about to get on a roll with Carol Ann, the front door opened and five women walked in, laughing and chatting. Each carried a bottle of wine. Jazzy Marie jumped off Brass's lap and ran to greet them

Chapter 6

ISABELLE HART

I sabelle sat on the curved copper bench tossing fish food to the koi that gobbled it up as it hit the water's surface. Feeding koi was a late afternoon habit she and Dan developed after the pond was built and one she continued after he died. Their graceful motion relaxed her and she needed that to shake off the cynical energy of the two detectives before going back upstairs.

Physically, Brass reminded Isabelle of her first serious boyfriend when she was a junior at Mount St. Mary and he was a sophomore at the University of Arkansas. Same height, weight, swagger, mischief in his green eyes, both played ball. She wondered if Brass was a good dancer too. She noticed the shadows change and remembered she needed to warm up the Mexico Chiquito Dip she'd prepared for her son's visit.

While the cheese dip heated, she picked up the file folder on her antique Chippendale writing desk. Her eyes fell on the snapshot in the narrow red lacquer frame that sat on the top. It was a photograph of her son, his two sisters, and herself standing in front of his yellow helicopter the day she picked up Dan's ashes from Ruebel Funeral Home. The four of them were getting ready to fly over the Arkansas River and scatter his incinerated crushed bones.

It had only been three years since he died, but it seemed like forever since that day. Her son recently learned he had bladder cancer, although it had been contained in the bladder, and the doctors at MD Anderson had assured him he was now clear. Still his cancer diagnosis was another trauma for the family. Her first husband, the father of her children, had died of kidney cancer not long before Dan was killed. Cancer death, accidental death, cancer scare, the betrayal of Warren Mitchell, the money he stole from her, detectives at her door, one thing after another. For so many years, the family had not experienced any sort of trauma, and now it seemed they were overrun by it.

Her son, smart, creative, ambitious, was a determined man. The doctors said he had beaten cancer, but her son didn't believe it. He'd told her several weeks earlier, after he couldn't complete the last ten miles of his seventy-five-mile bike ride, that he felt something was off in his body.

His physician at the famous cancer center, Nadir Kamat, told him that his fear that something had been missed was typical of cancer survivors. Her son wanted a body scan. Kamat said it wasn't necessary. He was cured. For his treatments in Houston, he took a private jet, spent four or five hours at the clinic, then headed back to Little Rock. His wife went with him. He'd spent more time with her during the six months of treatment than he had in the thirteen years they'd been married.

For the past two weeks, Isabelle had listened as her son played and replayed his worst fear of not living to see his seven- and nine-year-old children grow up. With his first set of children, now two women in their mid twenties, he'd been hands on and involved in every aspect of their lives. He was in his early twenties when they were born. After the divorce from their mother, the young girls lived with him most of the time. His current set of children, born when he was in his forties, hardly knew him. He spent most of his time growing his companies. With the diagnosis of cancer, he felt compelled to spend more time with his son, making up for lost time, but time is not recoverable.

Carley, his wife, was busy being a dance mom and completely caught up in her daughter Cici's dance lessons and competition. His daughter didn't seem to need him except for the money she wanted for the expensive dance costumes she required for her competitions. He'd even bought a Mercedes RV for Carley to haul Cici and her dance friends and their mountain of bags containing costumes, makeup, and whatever else they wanted, to their competitions.

Isabelle was thinking about the day she and her children had scattered Dan's ashes and how much had happened since, when she heard her son pull up in his new Cadillac CTS-V sedan. It could go from zero to sixty in less than four seconds. She was in the car when he hit the one hundred eighty-five mile an hour mark. The internal camera and microphone recorded the event. He drove like a man trying to kill himself, as he now flew his helicopter, and took risks on his mountain bike, dirt bike, and anything else with wheels. Her son had always been a risk taker but not like he was now. He was determined to feel every minute of life.

He walked in with the cellphone to his ear, talking away when he came up behind her. "Hi, Mom." Call finished, he tossed his cell on the counter, kissed her on the cheek as he walked past her to the refrigerator to take out two beers.

He handed Isabelle one, sat down in his favorite chair, and looked out at the river. She joined him and they sat saying nothing, watching the river run past, drinking their favorite brand of Belgian ale. Old style country music played in the background, Willie, Waylon, Kristofferson, Cash. He took a corn chip from the wooden Koa bowl and raked it across the hot cheese dip she'd set down on the table. "Spicy. Love it. Nobody makes it like you."

Then Toby Keith came on singing about justice and they both started smiling at the same time. Isabelle opened her laptop and handed it to him, along with another beer. It was a YouTube video of Warren Mitchell in Delphi Pond. He said, "Revenge is best enjoyed when the revenger witnesses the full effect," and Isabelle nodded in agreement.

Isabelle said, "I'm glad there are still men around who aren't afraid to live out the things Toby and Willie sing about. I wish I could thank them in person for what they did and making it public. Finally, that asshole got what he deserved."

Her son put his arms around her and gave her a long hug. "You tried, give yourself credit for that. I'm glad someone got the job done. Now you can move on. Love you, Moma."

Getting a little tipsy on beer, listening to country, bullshitting, and remembering was something they did a couple of times a month. It started right after Dan was killed and had become their habit.

Max stretched his back and walked to her desk. He ran his hand over the marquetry and admired the beautiful pieces of wood. He picked up the file folder containing the details of his newly created trust and began flipping through it until he reached the meat of it on page twenty, the rules Carley would have to live by if she wanted to collect her monthly check and yearly bonus from his trustee after he died.

"What do you think?" The grin on his face reminded Isabelle of herself.

"Smart move keeping this confidential from Carley." She waited a few seconds and said in a mock challenging tone, "Why don't you show it to her? Let her know you don't think she can manage a household and children without your supervision. Teach her to live on a budget. It's not like she grew up wealthy. If she hadn't of married you, she would still be living in her mother's house near the country club, selling real estate to her friends, and pretending she grew up rich on a farm down there in Stuttgart."

"Mom." It was the long drawn out "mom" that said he didn't want to talk about something. Carley was a topic they discussed with relish. But when Max wasn't in the mood, he would cut it off. Her son didn't like to acknowledge his mistakes and never made apologies to anyone. Carley was an error in judgment, something Max should have taken care of before his second child came along, but he hadn't. Isabelle often wondered why.

He had a provision for a trust protector, the person responsible for overseeing the trustee, and he had put Isabelle in the role. If Carley or the other beneficiaries disagreed with any of the decisions made by the trustee there was only one way to challenge him—the trust protector, aka Moma.

Isabelle said, "It looks like you are playing the hope-for-the-best-and-plan-for-the-worst game. If you drop dead in a week or two, you have ensured Carley is controlled by your trust for the rest of her life. If you find nothing has been overlooked in your body and you are clear of cancer as they claim, you already have financial things in order so she can't get a big chunk of your hard earned assets when you divorce her. That would be revenge you could witness, her living on a budget."

"Do you think it goes far enough?"

Isabelle snickered. "It's a masterpiece of control from the grave. I think if she knew about this, she would be hot with anger and divorce you today. Then at least she would have control over her personal life and her finances. I just hope this document is never needed. I envision you free of cancer and living a long life. I don't want my son to die before I do. Maybe I should go ahead and kill myself and break the curse. That way your sisters will be free of it. Four generations is enough."

"The Finn family curse. Tell me about the detectives," and she did.

"What's your feeling about Brass?"

"He's smart, even tempered, but that bitch of a partner is overconfident, easily riled, and full of attitude. Not good for a suspect to see this in a detective."

"I guess he will be paying me a visit sooner or later," he said scraping the last bit of hot dip out of the bowl.

Chapter 7

Detectives Bill Brass and Trudi Calasa

As they pulled out of the drive at the Twenty-Eight Hundred Club, Brass said, "I remember meeting Jim Bud Haley at a party given for the governor. Marshall Knight took me. Haley stood out physically, tall and lean, strong. He looked friendly and wore thick black-rimmed glasses. He covered up his savviness with a smidgen of good ole boy."

"I'll look him up on Google Images. Right now, I am starving and I need a good beer," Trudi said. "How about Big Orange?" So Brass turned right on Cantrell Road and then University. It was after five-thirty and the streets were busy as he searched for parking. Once inside Brass ordered himself a Duvel and the bartender sat a La Fin Du Monde in front of Trudi without her asking. She poured the bottle-fermented Canadian beer into a mug and let the head settle. Brass did the same with his beer. He picked up her bottle. "La Fin Du Monde, end of the world, haven't heard of it." Without asking he reached for her mug. Brass drew it under his nose like a crime scene analyst does when trying to detect a scent, and took a long slow sip. "I like it. How'd you know about it?"

"Greer. She went to Las Vegas with some of the professors. I guess they have every kind of beer on earth there. She recommended it to the owner of Big Orange and he started selling it. So you can thank her."

"I would except you've never introduced us."

"Maybe one of these days. Now let's talk about the widows."

"How about the one who got under your skin?" Brass liked digging at her. Trudi didn't bite.

She said, "It's incredible to me that these three women are such good and longtime friends when they are as different as the islands that make up Maui County. All that sappy Southern charm from Haley and Katz. The Hart woman, cold, she doesn't even try to be charming. The one thing they have in common is they controlled the interviews. I felt like a haole that just moved to Maui trying to talk to a local."

"What?" Brass often didn't get Trudi's references to her homeland culture.

"A white person is called a haole by native Hawaiians. Haoles that come for a vacation a couple of times, then buy a condo in Kihei or Wailea think they are in America, and well, they are as long as they stay in the resort areas or haole subdivisions. The more adventurous ones may get jobs as substitute teachers or volunteer at the art center in Makawao, take hula and learn to chant in Hawaiian, so they can learn the culture."

"What in hell are you talking about, Trudi?"

"Me and you, here in the South, are like haoles who try to fit in when they move to Maui. The aloha spirit, Southern hospitality, tourist talk. Southern people and Hawaiians are alike in that they put a smile on their faces and offer you a welcoming spirit but you will never be one of them, no matter how hard you try. I know about fucking with outsiders and that's what we are to those women."

"That was intense. Should we back off and give this case to one of the detectives who grew up around here?"

"Never! I am saying we can't take one word these widows have said as the truth. I know they are hiding something, I feel it."

Brass felt it too. "I'll put Kristin on it. In a couple of hours she'll have the background on all three of them." He looked down at his phone and sent a text.

Kristin Gilmore was once the best paralegal in Arkansas. When her boss, prominent trust attorney Dick McCoy, retired, she could have made twice her salary working for the big old law firms. Instead, she went to work for Brass as his personal assistant. McCoy had practiced alone and Kristin wasn't interested in getting tangled up in the politics of a big Little Rock firm, no matter how great the money.

She met Brass shortly after his move from Colorado. Chief Knight recommended to Brass that he reach out to Dick McCoy when a complex trust issue regarding his sister came up. It was the start of his friendship with McCoy and Kristin. He respected the lawyer, old school, a man with integrity, one who could make his case in one page when it took others thirty. McCoy was the opposite of the breed of attorney who didn't really practice law. The kind who practiced the art of ruining the reputations of those they brought lawsuits against.

As the waiter set down their sandwiches, Brass's phone vibrated and he listened without taking a bite. Trudi was halfway through her meal by the time he finished.

"Kristin's already started on it. Her anticipation is astounding. McCoy said that was one of the things that made her better than all the lawyers he went up against, anticipation. She'll get back to me on it."

"The widows have motive, but Isabelle Hart is the obvious choice," Trudi said. "I am going with that for now."

"If they are responsible, someone else would have to be involved. I can't see those women trussing up Mitchell and anchoring him to a hunk of concrete. Katz and Haley say they've forgiven Mitchell, but that could be lies. I'd say they have the imagination, especially Hart. Maybe someone knew the widows were going to Delphi and put Mitchell in the pond after the women got there. When he was discovered, the widows would be blamed. I have another idea . . ."

Trudi held up her hand to stop him. "I get the picture, but the simplest answer is probably the best. Hart did it. I don't see someone accidentally finding out and using the widows as a cover."

"Well, Trudi. We don't know how many people knew the widows were planning their Halloween gig at Delphi. Just maybe, one of them hired someone to carry out the plan and the other two didn't know. Who says they had to act as a unit? The psychic knew they were going to be at Delphi that night. That type is probably an artery of information. Or maybe Carol Ann told her hairdresser, or Brenda told hers, Hart doesn't look like she spends much time in a salon, or maybe Carol Ann told someone at the Twenty-Eight Hundred Club, or Brenda Katz told someone from her bridge club. Southerners are known gossipers."

Trudi indicated to the waiter she wanted the dessert menu.

"Isabelle Hart is going to have to answer a few more questions in the morning, but I don't want you there. You go see Katz, first thing."

"Maybe I should have a session with Laurel Moon, psychic to the Little Rock Police Department. How many cases has she helped you guys solve?" Trudi rolled her eyes as she said it.

"Not a bad idea."

"You're kidding."

"Make an appointment, Trudi. Go undercover and channel your inner kahuna."

"Do you even know what a kahuna is?"

"Magic Man? Witch doctor? Healer? I don't know."

"As this case gets stranger, so do you, Brass."

"I have been down here in Arkansas for a few years now. I guess it's rubbing off."

Brass's phone pinged again. It was a text from Kristin. *Going to get a session with Moon. Thought we might learn something. That okay?*

Brass smiled at Trudi. "Never mind about Moon. Kristin is taking care of it, anticipatory genius."

"You're saying you didn't ask her and she came up with that on her own?"

"I am."

Trudi wanted to say she'd thought of visiting Moon herself so why didn't he call her an anticipatory genius, but she didn't. She felt competitive with

Kristin and made a conscious effort to hide it. Most of the work Kristin did for Brass involved searches on background for his scripts, corresponding with his agent, things to do with his other career. Kristin would have made a great detective.

Chapter 8

JIM BUD HALEY

J im Bud Haley was born in Hot Springs, Arkansas. Bath House Row, Oaklawn Racetrack, and gambling identified the resort town back then. His daddy a lawyer, his mother a nurse, his aunt managed the Majestic Bath House. Uncle Colter was a bookie, but Jim Bud wanted to be like his uncle Jim, his mother's oldest brother, a firefighter.

By the time Jim Bud was sixteen he was six feet four inches of pure muscle, handsome, a boy who looked and acted older than his years. When Sherry, his younger sister by two years, was fourteen she was raped and beaten by the son of a prominent local man, and Jim Bud urged her to speak up and accuse him.

So she did—only to become a victim of the tyranny of gossip by the way her attacker's lawyer defined her. The case never got to court and Sherry Haley left Hot Springs and went to live with her mother's older sister and her family in Memphis.

Jim Bud didn't see her again until she was in her coffin at a funeral home in Memphis. She finished high school in Tennessee, went to nursing school, and worked as a nurse. On the tenth anniversary of her attack, after her shift ended,

Sherry went into a restroom on the floor where she worked and injected an opiate into her rectum and it killed her.

After he got his law degree, Jim Bud moved to Little Rock and started out as a prosecutor, until he realized there was no power in the position, so he followed his father's advice and went into contract law.

He'd been divorced from a state senator's daughter for a few years when Carol Ann came into his life. It was a friendly divorce, she'd found a rich man from Georgia to marry and that was fine with Jim Bud. Hostility toward her wouldn't have gotten him anywhere. Friends like the senator were more important than anger at an ex-wife.

When Carol Ann walked into his office with a swollen eye and a broken jaw applying for a job as his secretary, she got his attention. He could see underneath the damage she was a beautiful woman. Carol Ann told Jim Bud she wanted to divorce her husband and needed a job first. "I have a liberal arts degree from Fayetteville, no experience at anything except being a wife and mother, but I am smart, I work hard, and I get what I want."

When Jim Bud asked why she wanted a divorce, Carol Ann said, "He hit me one too many times so I got even. Now it's time to leave and take my two kids."

Jim Bud was curious about what she considered getting even and asked.

"I was frying chicken, he was sitting at the kitchen table with his shirt off, and I accidentally dropped the skillet of hot grease on his back. He's in the hospital right now in the burn unit."

Jim Bud gave her the job, got her the divorce, and they married a year later and stayed that way for over thirty. Around the state, Jim Bud and Carol Ann were known as the couple with connections. If you were a politician, or wanted to be, they were on your get- to-know list.

By the time he was fifty, Jim Bud's friends ranged from the governor to convicted felons. He had a knack for moving between the layers of society and the range of his friendships proved it. It wasn't a good day for him when the governor of Arkansas became president of the United States. It brought too much scrutiny on him and he lost his law license for a year over a financial scandal which involved the former governor.

Due to his lifestyle and his career, Jim Bud could not openly practice the kind of law he preferred, getting abused women the justice they deserved. Little Rock was a small town, and if he represented the wife of a prominent man who wore bruises under her designer clothes, he would not get invitations to the parties he wanted to attend or introductions to the people he needed to meet. So the Haleys found another way.

Carol Ann usually brought the case to Jim, and he contacted an old friend who'd made this type of law his specialty. Jim worked behind the scenes and sometimes paid the attorney's fee himself if the woman didn't have the money. If the courts failed her, unknown forces came into play.

If a chronic wife beater wasn't held accountable, in a year or so, he might be assaulted and humiliated, or worse. If he liked to run for exercise, his Achilles tendon might be severed. If his sport was biking he might tumble off his bike on the river trail in North Little Rock and find himself in the river where he might not be found.

Battered women married to prominent or wealthy men don't usually take their problems to court but rather to a friend. The lucky ones found themselves at the Twenty-Eight-Hundred Club. Carol Ann was a good listener. Many times they showed up at five in the afternoon with a bottle of wine, or vodka, often it was gin, and a stiff neck, or bruised hips, abdominal bruises, or other hidden injuries. Sooner or later, the husband suffered either a physically or financially debilitating injury, or blackmail.

Jim Bud's clients often asked him to keep things safe for them. He would give the client a metal box and tell him or her to place whatever it was inside and lock it. He didn't want to know what was in there. He kept these boxes in his private office at home. Jim Bud knew how to open all sorts of locks.

Jim Bud kept files on every important person in Arkansas: senators, judges, governors, stockbrokers, bankers, sheriffs, police chiefs, prison superintendents, anyone who had any kind of power in the state. He liked to think, relatively speaking, his files rivaled those J. Edgar Hoover kept on his friends, enemies, and everyone else he considered important. The files were Jim Bud's bargaining tools and his insurance policies.

Jim Bud's plane planted its nose into the runway at North Little Rock airfield when he was at the top of his game, and the loss of him reverberated throughout the entire state and perhaps beyond.

When Carol Ann got the call two detectives were coming to question her about Warren Mitchell, she felt the weight of Jim Bud and their secrets on her shoulders. Without him, she felt unprotected and alone. She missed sleeping next to him the most.

After Brass and Calasa left and the Club members went home, Carol Ann gathered up years of history, the files, the boxes, the evidence of all the good they'd done, from his home office and packed it up.

Carol Ann looked at herself in the mirror. Her hair, her expensive clothes, her congenial persona. She picked up her purse, took her revolver out, removed five of the six bullets, spun the cylinder, put it up to her head. She'd been playing the spin game on and off since Jim Bud died. She wondered if this would be the time her luck ran out, then she squeezed the trigger.

Chapter 9

KRISTIN GILMORE AND THE PSYCHIC

Laurel Moon lived out on the old Hot Springs Highway about twenty minutes from the Little Rock City limits on a two lane road lined by ancient trees. The drive itself was a trip into the past. Small brick and frame houses built back in the thirties sat fifty feet from the road on large wooded lots with natural landscaping, no mulch or Bradford pears.

Kristin turned right onto the gravel drive and pulled into the parking lot. The house, constructed of buff brick, was shaded by a tremendous oak that cast its branches over the house like a protector. Nothing about it indicated a psychic lived there, no moons and stars hanging from the branches, nary a gargoyle guarded the entrance. It was the kind of place so indistinctive it was nearly invisible.

Kristin parked her white Lexus next to the only car in the lot, an old Ford pickup which hadn't moved in so many years it looked like yard art. Moon scheduled her appointments with thirty minutes in between to give herself time to recover from her trips into the ether and to give clients enough time between appointments that they wouldn't run into each other. There was no charge for the visits; however, clients were expected to make "donations" and place the cash on a plate by the front door when they left. For telephone and internet sessions, it was PayPal. The recommended donation was a hundred dollars for forty-five minutes.

Kristin gently rapped on the door and a chubby woman dressed in a pair of black slacks and a billowy, long-sleeved yellow blouse opened the door. Her clothing suggested daylight and dark, the sun above the ample waist and the night below. Her gray and brown curly hair fell to her shoulders. Her jewelry was one silver moon and the other a silver star dangling from her ears. She looked to be close to sixty.

"Hello, Kristin. Please, remove your shoes and leave them on the porch." Her voice was warm while her blue-green eyes were appraising.

Kristin did and stepped into her entrance hall and that was as far as she got. Laurel Moon stood between her and the living room where she held her sessions. Kristin saw a large, round glass table set on top of a polished cedar stump with cushions on the floor for seating. Kristin thought of a Kidididi's restaurant, where you had to be flexible enough to get down on the floor and back up if you wanted to eat there.

A pack of cards, two small bottles of water, and a large crystal sat on the table. The room was painted soft orange and it seemed to glow from the indirect lighting. Along the back wall, under two windows, sat a cream suede sectional sofa and a matching chair across from it. There were no curtains on the windows. The shrubbery grew so close that it acted as window coverings, encasing the room like a womb.

Moon did not take appointments without a referral from an existing client. Kristin's friend Sharon had called the psychic on her behalf. They stood facing each other while Kristin waited for Laurel Moon to invite her inside. Instead, she took Kristin's hands in hers, closed her eyes, and held that position. When she spoke, her words astounded Kristin.

"You are toxic. It would be unwise of me to let you enter into my sacred space unless you are purified. I must ask you to leave unless you agree to a cleansing."

Sharon had not mentioned this part, and it put Kristin on edge. She hesitated and was unsure whether to pull her hands from Moon's grip or not. Kristin hoped the woman had not felt the small rigor that passed through her body upon hearing the terms.

"Toxic?" Kristin, a good six inches taller than Moon, looked down at the woman. "What do you mean by that?" She hoped her voice wasn't too stern.

"Your energy is very unsettling to me. I cannot work with you in your current state. It would make me ill." She let go of Kristin's hands, stepped back away from her, and folded her arms in front of her chest. Kristin recognized it as a protective posture.

"Do you think I have a communicable disease or something?" Kristin laughed to show she was joking because she didn't know how to react. When she was unsure, kidding was her go-to response.

"You know better. It is your spirit that is sick. I can help, if you will allow me."

"Cleanse?" It sounded perverted. Carnival tricksters was how she classified fortune tellers, psychics, tarot card and palm readers. The thing that brought her here was Brass. He was great at what he did, a sincere person, good hearted, McCoy liked him, and she wanted to help him, to do whatever it is older sisters do to help their little brothers. She had one of these, a younger brother—he was an ass.

"I will explain and you decide if you want to continue. I ask that you remove all your garments. You will stand in a bath that contains salts, oils, and herbs that will draw the physical toxicity out of your body. I will use fire to cleanse your spirit. Do not worry. I am not going to burn you. I will surround your body with a healing smoke. While I am doing this you will recite the Lord's Prayer out loud repeatedly until I am finished. Then I will provide you with a robe and we can begin on your journey. Agreed?"

Kristin hesitated.

"Well, then, we are finished." Moon indicated the outer door.

"N-no." Kristin stuttered a little when she spoke again. "I was surprised." Pause. "I've never been to a psychic. Yes. I agree." The last thing Kristin wanted was for Moon to kick her out. Getting naked in front of this woman would take her out of her comfort zone, yet something inside of her told her to go for it. Her birthday was in a couple of days and maybe a cleansing would be a good start to her personal new year. She was thinking about taking up yin yoga. It was supposed to be the best kind for women over fifty.

"Then we will get started. Put your garments in this basket." Laurel gestured toward the inner room after Kristin was totally nude. The psychic handed her a beach towel and Kristin wrapped it around herself. "Come on in. I will wash up and we will begin."

When Laurel Moon returned, Kristin almost didn't recognize her. She wore a purple velvet robe, her hair was braided in a crown around her head. The braid dripped with crystals and other shiny stones that were woven into it. Kristin thought it must be a wig. Moon looked as if she had just stepped out of a costume shop. Kristin knew some of Moon's clients and could not imagine even one of them coming way out here seeking advice or whatever they wanted from Moon and getting naked to do it. She thought about grabbing her clothes and running. She felt Moon was trying to establish control over her.

Moon carried a device that looked like the foot bath for a home pedicure kit, plugged it in, added water, and a packet of something pungent smelling and told Kristin to drop the towel and stand in it. As she stood in the hot bubbling water, Laurel Moon poured accelerant over some herbs into a ceramic bowl and lit it. The flame jumped up and then settled down. She told Kristin to start reciting the Lord's Prayer and then proceeded to make circles around her with her scented fire bowl, chanting, or talking in tongues, Kristin didn't know.

When finished, Moon told Kristin to step out and sprayed her with aromatic oil that felt like it was permeating her cells to the bone. Kristin could feel it in her lungs and feared for a moment the woman had poisoned her, but settled herself. Moon handed her a scented robe to put on and indicated with her chubby hand for Kristin to sit on one of the cushions placed around the table.

Moon spread the tarot cards out across the table with one swipe reminding Kristin of a card dealer in Vegas and told her to pick one. She chose the last one and Moon flipped it over. The Death card.

"You are the keeper of secrets that are killing you, emotionally, and spiritually. You need to confess them to those who need to know them and free yourself from this burden."

Moon asked if she had brought a favored object with her. When Kristin nodded, Moon held out her hand as Kristin removed the bear claw from around her neck. She had gotten it in Montana that past summer and had worn it nearly every day since. Moon clasped her short fingers around it. "Now, tell me what it is you want from me."

Kristin knew this question was coming and had thought of many things to say, now all of them seemed inadequate. She winged it.

"I want to talk about getting justice."

"You mean revenge."

"My financial advisor robbed me of my savings. I think I'm due some retribution."

Moon closed her eyes and, still holding the claw, she put her hands in her lap. Minutes passed in silence.

Kristin expected to tell Moon the story of how her dead husband's financial advisor had befriended her, how she'd trusted him, and he'd betrayed her by stealing her inheritance. She didn't expect Moon to go into a trance.

"You are not being honest with me," Moon whispered, and opened her eyes locking them with Kristin's.

Kristin felt a chill go through her. Before she could speak, Laurel Moon closed her eyes again and held the bear claw against her chest. Her voice was quiet and Kristin was barely able to hear her words when she spoke.

"You use your intellect to trap and control. Your current way of life will soon be finished, and then you will experience a rebirth if you are willing to let your old ways die. As I hold the claw of this bear which you have worn for many months, I see that you are going to have to claw your way out of your bad habits. It won't be easy."

Laurel laid the bear claw on the table with a clank, uncrossed her legs and used the edge of the table to help herself rise from her sitting position, then left the room. Kristin dressed and went looking for Laurel Moon. She found her in the bathroom taking off her wig. Kristin, tall, athletic, and strong, towered over Laurel. She grabbed her by the shoulders and turned Moon around to face her. She gave the short, chubby woman a hearty shake. "You are a fucking fraud."

That, Kristin thought, felt good, but it didn't feel like her. She could not recall ever confronting someone in a physical way like she'd just done and wondered if the toxic release had stirred up something inside of her that had been hiding deep down and was now emerging. Her whole body zinged and she felt a little like she would start laughing. She wondered what Dick McCoy would think if he saw her now, or Brass.

Kristin snapped up the empty silver collection plate on her way out and slammed the front door. As soon as she pulled out of the lot, she called Sharon. "What the fuck, Sharon! I had to strip down and take a bath in fire for her to speak to me. Why didn't you tell me that was going to happen!"

Sharon said it didn't sound like Laurel at all, and she didn't know of anyone who had ever been made to go through what Kristin did. "For heaven's sake, Kristin, why didn't you leave? Why did you do it? Didn't you think it sounded perverted?"

She said only, "I thought it was a requirement."

Kristin couldn't wait to tell her story to Brass and punched in his number as soon as she turned onto the highway. "Moon called me at nine last night. She said that she'd just had a cancellation and that was the only opening she would have for a month so I took it. I was at her place first thing this morning. I stayed up late researching Mitchell and the widows. I should have texted you about the appointment and emailed the background on the widows, but I didn't have time."

Trudi listened on speaker as Kristin described in detail her experience with the psychic. Trudi couldn't imagine stripping naked and saying prayers. She would not have done it.

"What did the friend tell Moon about Kristin?" Trudi asked Brass when the call had ended.

"Gave Moon her name. Said they'd been friends for years and Kristin was working as a researcher for a writer but she didn't know who. Said Kristin wanted to talk about her future." Brass laughed until he snorted. "I am trying to imagine Kristin and that whole scene. She's going to spend the rest of the day on Laurel and the Moon family. When she gets something in her craw, she works on it until she spits it out."

"God, Brass, you sound like a hillbilly."

"Just trying on the local language for size."

"What did she say about the widows?"

"Said her background was not finished. She is meticulous and doesn't want to say anything until the job is complete. Said she needed more on all of them. Only had the bare bones. Here is what I had to beg for. Finn was Isabelle Hart's maiden name. She grew up here, went to Catholic schools, married two days after her eighteenth birthday. Had three kids, married Hart a week after her divorce. Was getting info on her ex and would let me know. She was Hart's third wife. Seventeen years younger than him and they just had their thirtieth anniversary when he was killed.

"Dan Hart was a commercial contractor, small shopping centers, things like that. He bought the old Penal Farm property and some of the surrounding land and turned it into the subdivision where Isabelle Hart lives. Dan's parents owned one of those historic hotels in the downtown area and some office buildings. His family has been in Little Rock four generations. Isabelle Finn's father died when she was a child. Private plane crash in the 1950s. Like her husband. Funny how that works. Her mother started working as a bookkeeper for an architect and her grandmother raised her and her siblings. She has that in common with Carol Ann Haley, the crash and the father dying young.

"Hart left everything directly to Isabelle even though he had four kids by his first two wives. Mitchell was Dan Hart's financial advisor. After Hart's death she relied on Mitchell. They talked once a week or more."

Trudi frowned. "She was the only investor who brought a lawsuit against him and she filed a couple of FINRA complaints too."

Brass nodded. "The Katz and Haley stories are pretty much the same as Hart's regarding Mitchell. He introduced the three women to some of his divorced male clients. Brenda Katz is the only one who started dating one of them and that was Dennis Moon, also a victim."

"Moon. That's an odd name. Any relation to Laurel? I thought that was probably a made up name she used in her psychic business. Now a Dennis Moon," Trudi commented, making a notation on her legal pad.

"I thought so too. Kristin will look into it. Anyway, the widows have been friends since grade school, went to the same high school. Brenda Katz might seem like an old hippie but she is a CPA and worked with her husband at his firm. Isabelle Hart has a degree in botany. She started college after her children were born. Hart set her up in a business growing orchids and other exotic plants after they married. Carol Ann is clever and good at introducing people who need each other, a fixer type. Oh, she was also runner-up to Miss Arkansas one year and won Miss Congeniality, and she was a Razorback homecoming queen."

Trudi said, "All that background is great but it wouldn't have made a difference in my chat with Katz this morning. What about you and Hart?"

"I agree. Here's what I got." Brass turned on video of his interview, put his feet up, and closed his eyes, while Trudi watched Isabelle Hart's body language and listened.

When it was over Trudi remarked, "You didn't waste any time accusing her of being the mastermind. Why?"

"Surprise. Hoped to shake her up, soften her a little."

"She didn't seem surprised or intimidated." Trudi rolled her eyes upward and repeated Hart's words. " 'If you had evidence I am responsible, then you would charge me.' "

"I expected her to walk out of the room instead she sat there. At least I learned something new or perhaps she pointed out something I missed would be more accurate."

Trudi scrolled back. "Are you talking about her long speech? It sounded practiced to me." She pushed play and Isabelle Hart's voice filled the room.

"Detective Brass, you asked me several times if I heard anything, and I said no, yet you don't believe me. Apparently, you are not aware there is construction work on Cantrell at nights. They are digging up parts of the highway and putting down pipe. It makes a racket, lots of trucks coming and going. We brought headphones to cancel out their noise and listen to chants. The crew was working when we got there. Lights, big equipment, flaggers, the whole business. The fog hadn't set in yet. Once it hung down over the road, I guess they stopped work. Evidently, they were gone when your team arrived.

"As for the seeing, if you walked the perimeter of Delphi, you would know on that side where we had our camp those cattails are thick and tall. The only reason we saw the hunter was he came charging right through them toward us. So now you can quit asking me the same questions."

Trudi commented, "For her that was a lot of talking. When I arrived at the pond, there was no one on the job. Here is the name of the company. I was going to check on it. Unless you would prefer Kristin do it." Brass noticed the acid comment. She handed him a slip of paper with the name BigRock Construction and the contact information. "So that's the only new thing you got from Hart. Roadwork. What's your read on her after seeing her a second time?"

"Pretty much the same. A woman of few words, careful, practiced, consistent, likes to tease and toy for the pleasure of it. She knows more than she's telling. I just haven't asked the right questions yet. After the interview, I feel even more strongly she's the instigator; she had help, just not sure if Katz and Haley knew and are protecting her. It is hard for three people to keep the same secret. When I talk to Mitchell, I'll get a better idea."

Trudi said, "I asked Katz how they were able to subdue a man Mitchell's size. She looked right at me and laughed, told me I had a big imagination." Trudi imitated Katz, " 'Honey, if you had proof of that, you'd be here with handcuffs. I have better things to do with my morning than listen to silly suppositions. Now, don't let the screen door hit you in the ass on your way out.' "

Brass chuckled. "Where was she headed, to another event at the grandkids' school?"

"No. She works as an accountant. Started doing that again after the CD loss. When she answered the door, I wasn't sure it was her at first. She wasn't dressed like a hippy and she'd dropped the heavy Southern drawl. She wore a dark suit that looked expensive, high heels, and her hair was pulled back. If I had been fifteen minutes later, I would have missed her.

"I did get her robe. I told her I needed it to eliminate her as the person who fired the shot and she told me I could go down into the basement and look for it. It was on top of a mountain of dirty clothes. The lab has it.

"Haley isn't answering her phone. I called several times. Went by there after I saw Katz, her car was parked in front. The little dog didn't start yapping when I rang the bell. I thought she might have taken it for a walk and drove around the neighborhood. Went around the entire house, backyard, looked in windows, and nothing. I called Katz and asked if she had a key to Haley's place, said maybe something was wrong, and asked her to meet me there. Katz said Haley probably wanted to be left alone and would surface by five. What do you think?"

Brass looked at his watch. "Let's go see Warren Mitchell. He should be up to a visit by now. Then you check back on Haley."

Chapter 10

WARREN MITCHELL
MEETS THE DETECTIVES

B rass opened the door to Warren Mitchell's hospital room. He appeared to be asleep, as did the woman sitting next to his bed with her head back against the chair snoring with her mouth open. She reminded him of a passenger on an all-night flight in coach.

Brass watched the man. He wasn't sleeping, his eyes were moving beneath his lids, pretending sleep. Brass gave him a little shake on the leg to startle him. "Sorry to wake you."

Mitchell opened his eyes with a start. "What?" He blinked several times. "Who are you?" His voice sounded groggy. Brass didn't buy it.

"I am Detective Brass and this is my partner, Detective Calasa. We are working on finding the person or persons responsible for putting you in this bed."

"Sorry. Give me a minute. You woke me from a dead sleep." He rubbed his hand across his face and massaged his scalp vigorously with his fingertips.

Mitchell, a tall man, took up the entire length of the bed. Brass guessed him to be about six foot five and two hundred seventy-five pounds. His thick brown hair was showing a little gray.

The woman in the chair didn't wake and Brass was inclined to let her be, but Mitchell called her name, "Judy. Judy. Wake up. The police are here." She jerked her head forward, eyes blurry. It took her a minute to collect herself and then she stood and introduced herself.

Trudi explained, "Ma'am, we are detectives working on the case. I am Trudi Calasa and this is Bill Brass. How about you and I go down to the Starbucks in the food court and have some coffee and maybe bring some back for the men." Trudi gave her best Southern hospitality imitation to make Judy feel comfortable.

The women left and Brass got to the point. "Do you have any idea who did this to you?"   He didn't play around with liars and instinct told him he was looking at one. Best not to give Mitchell time to get into a rhythm.

Mitchell said he didn't have a clue.

"What about your clients? The ones who lost millions. Any one of them come to mind?"

Mitchell touched the bed control and brought the head up. "Most of my clients stuck with me. I was lied to by Stanford. I am a victim myself and so is my family. My mother lost everything and she is living with us now. I am supporting her as best I can, considering my ability to get new clients has been impaired."

"Why is that?"

"Isabelle Hart is the main reason. She filed a lawsuit against me. It didn't go anywhere because the Stanford Receiver put a stop to it. She made several complaints with FINRA, not only about the CDs but other stocks and bonds I sold her. It was in the local papers and all over the internet. Now her complaints pop up anytime someone goes to the BrokerCheck on their website. That has made a huge impact."

"You think Isabelle Hart is responsible."

"She is an unforgiving woman. The only thing I am guilty of is trying to do the best that I could for my clients and being naive. Stanford fooled me like he did many brokers. I am guilty of that. I admit it. I have asked my Lord Jesus Christ to forgive me and the pain I have caused others, and he has."

"Besides Isabelle Hart, how many clients did you lose?"

"Three. My biggest worry is Judy, not clients. She has cancer, you know. We have been fighting it for five years. She is in remission now but we worry from checkup to checkup that it will come back on us."

Brass couldn't understand it when men talked in the "we" when it came to their wives being pregnant or having cancer. "We are pregnant." Every time he heard that he wanted to puke. In his mind, there was no "we" about it. "Try and think. Who else comes to mind?"

"My mind is not working. You're saying that you think what happened to me is related to the Stanford mess?"

"It is an obvious motive, maybe not the actual one. We need to investigate all the possibilities. Do you know a Carol Ann Haley?"

"Yes, I do. Why?"

"Is she a client?"

"She stuck with me. Moved half of her assets and kept the rest with me. Why do you ask about her?"

"Doing a background on the Stanford victims and read a story about her husband's accident."

"Carol Ann is a wonderful woman."

Trudi returned to the room. She walked over to Mitchell and touched his arm. "Judy's gone home to get cleaned up. Said she would be back in a couple of hours." She handed Brass his espresso.

"Warren, what do you remember before you were kidnapped?" Trudi asked as she took Judy's chair and scooted it close to the bed and took Mitchell's hand in hers. "I know those kinds of memories can be pretty upsetting; please, go back to that time."

Brass couldn't believe his eyes. Trudi being gentle, supportive, whatever it was she was doing holding Mitchell's hand and looking concerned.

Mitchell broke out in tears. Trudi patted his forearm and cut her eyes at Brass indicating he should step back from the bed and out of Mitchell's view. She wanted Mitchell to focus on her.

"That's just it. I can't remember anything. I don't remember going home after work, I don't remember leaving the office. The last thing I remember is seeing a new client. I stayed late to meet her. She came to sign documents I had prepared to open her account and to transfer her existing accounts, and I can't remember anything after that."

"Let's begin with her. How did she contact you? Start there and simply tell what you remember. We have plenty of time. She may or may not be important, but, remembering her might open up other memories for you. Now take a moment and start when you are ready," Trudi coached.

"Several months ago, I got a call from Jana McKeller. She said she was moving to Little Rock. Her husband had recently died of a heart attack and her daughter wanted her to move into their guest house in Hickory Hill. She had been living there for several months to decide if she wanted to move to Little Rock and decided she did.

"Jana said she had been attending the church where my family and I go. She said Pastor John advised her to call me. He told her what I had been going through and that because of it, I would be more careful with her funds than someone who had not suffered as I have. She said she read Isabelle Hart's complaints about me on BrokerCheck. It didn't worry her. She agreed with Pastor John about how a tragedy can strengthen a person.

"I talked with her several times over the phone and liked her, and as I said, new clients have been hard to come by. I talked to Pastor John and he told me she was a lovely woman and had made a generous contribution to the children's playground. Her worth is around four million so she was qualified. We don't accept clients unless they have a net worth of at least one million.

"We made arrangements to meet at six on October thirty-first. My receptionist waited until Jana arrived and left after she brought her to my office. She looked to be in her sixties, I would say. She used a cane otherwise she seemed to be in good health. She was well dressed, wore glasses, and had the kind of way about her that many older ladies have. She brought me a gift, which surprised me. I am a Woodford Reserve man and she brought a bottle along with these delicious handmade chocolates with bourbon centers.

"She signed the papers and we celebrated with a little of the Woodford and a couple of the chocolates. I might have had at least four." He patted his stomach. "I've gained a little around the middle. My doctor tells me it is normal when someone has gone through what I have. The rest is a blank. A dark blank."

"Tell me, Warren, after the signing and the celebration, do you recall Jana leaving your office?"

He shut his eyes and hung his head. "No. Wait. I am seeing it now. I now remember. I was in the water; I couldn't move. My hands were bound up. I could see. I felt someone holding me around my waist. A man said . . . what was it? 'Warren, can you hear me?' and I nodded. He said, something scary like, 'You will live as long as you stand. If you stay floating long enough maybe someone will find you.' Then he was gone. I'd forgotten that until just now. And a little while later a girl on a surfboard came up to me. At first I thought I had imagined her, but she was real. I don't remember anything else until I woke up in the emergency room."

Warren Mitchell looked exhausted and the detectives knew they wouldn't get any more out of him. "Warren. Get some sleep," Trudi said and patted his arm. "After you've had some rest, we will talk again." Trudi rose from Judy's chair and walked toward Brass. Her eyes said, *Keep your mouth shut.* "If you think of anything else, call me. I left my card with Judy. Take care now."

They left the room and closed the door. "You being Miss Supportive, what was that about? Did I just witness the aloha spirit?"

"I learned a few things about our boy from Judy over coffee and a couple of pastries. He needs a lot of stroking so I gave him what he needed. Got a problem with that?" Trudi grinned. "Didn't think so. We should stop by his office and have a look at the documents, have the techs go over the place. What do you want to bet the papers aren't there?"

"Jana McKeller was a setup? Is that what you are thinking?" Brass asked.

"Only one way to find out. I think we need to make sure they do a complete screen on his blood and look for something besides chocolate and bourbon."

Brass and Trudi drove out to Mitchell's office. The receptionist remembered meeting Jana McKeller and described her the same as Mitchell had. His assistant could not find any record of the signed documents or a box of chocolates or a bottle of Woodford.

Trudi said, "I believe parts of his story, not all of it. It doesn't follow that he can't remember anything after seeing Blue. Cole wrapped that light around his neck. He pulled off the tape from his mouth. I don't buy it. What I can't figure is his motive for holding back."

Brass asked, "Have you heard about people who pay big bucks to have someone kidnap them or do other things, so they can feel the thrill of it all? As I understand it, that sort of thing is on the rise, especially among the really rich. Do you think Mitchell could be into something like that?"

"No. He doesn't need any more attention drawn to himself. I don't know if you've been on the local blogs, but whoever did this had someone out there recording it all." She got out her iPhone. "I am sending you a couple of the links. In my opinion, this was about torture and disgrace. If you were his client and saw this, I bet you would find a new financial advisor."

Trudi looked up from her phone. "I'm going to try and locate Haley again. What about you?"

"Going to drive out to BigRock Construction. See what the night foreman on the job has to say."

Chapter 11

Chapter 11

DETECTIVE BRASS
MEETS MAX WALKER

Brass pulled up to BigRock Construction's main gate. The low structures scattered over several acres were surround by wire and beyond the fencing the flat ground was covered in gravel. The place reminded him of a prison. The metal buildings were all painted caution yellow, as was the equipment, and the shirts of the employees he saw walking around the yard were the same shade.

The guard, dressed in a BigRock uniform, yellow shirt and jeans, required a photo ID before he hit the button to open the electronic gate. Brass noticed the security camera mounted on top of the station. He was directed to a one-story metal building straight in front of him.

Brass walked up the steps and stood at the entrance, looking around at the vast amount of heavy equipment. The concrete and asphalt plants were going full force. Mountains of crushed rock, asphalt, and old concrete made him think of a quarry. He felt like he had landed on a raw planet that was in the process of being constructed. Trucks came and went, men moved around, and a helicopter the same yellow as the other equipment set down behind a cluster of buildings close to the back perimeter.

The heavy metal door didn't open when Brass turned the knob. A voice came over the intercom and asked his name and then he heard a buzzer as the door unlocked. He was expecting to be met by an armed guard but instead found himself in a waiting room with a young African American woman sitting behind a desk.

On the wall to her left sat an antique French baker's cabinet and over it an oil painting of a man standing in front of a giant redwood, his right leg was bent backward with his booted foot resting against the trunk. The inscription beneath the painting read, "Manny Walker, to whom this building is dedicated."

Brass thought he was having a hallucination: Manny, his Manny, Wye Mountain Manny. Brass's hand touched the belt buckle. A mural of an American Indian tribe in a camp was painted on the opposite wall. Underneath was a long bench made of steel, leather, and buffalo skin. Brass was so overloaded that he didn't hear the receptionist speak. When he finally did, he saw her hold up an index finger to indicate he wait as she took a call.

His phone pinged at the same time. Trudi. The text read, *Nah Nah Nah*. He figured "nah" meant "ha" in her home tongue. She had done the background on BigRock. The rest of her text read, *Forgot to mention that Max Walker, the owner of BigRock, is Manny's son with Isabelle Finn Walker Hart.*

The receptionist asked Brass to wait a few minutes. The appointment was with the foreman on the Cantrell Road job but that was not the man who walked toward him. He was maybe five foot nine and wore khaki pants and the BigRock shirt. His hair, a medium brown with a little sprinkling of gray, was cut short. He walked full of confidence and it was obvious he was in great physical shape. He held out his hand before he reached Brass and introduced himself. To Brass his resemblance to his mother was uncanny. He wondered if it bothered Max Walker, a man in his late forties, that he had not reached the six foot three height of his father. He did have Manny's blue eyes that looked out at Brass with his mother's challenging directness.

Walker shook Brass's hand and introduced himself. "Mom told me you were wearing the buckle."

Brass didn't respond. He cursed Trudi as he felt his right hand move to touch it and stopped himself.

"Come back to my office," Max said as he turned and walked away.

Brass followed him through a maze of hallways to an office that to him didn't say "owner." It was a corner room with windows looking out in two directions. Three monitors sat on the desk, unrolled plans on another, white boards with job descriptions hung on the walls. There was absolutely nothing personal in the office, nothing that spoke of a family or hobbies.

"You want to know about the work on the night of the thirty-first out on Cantrell Road near Delphi Pond. I have Troy's report." He handed it to Brass and indicated a chair for him to sit. "Look it over. I'll answer your questions about the work." Walker sat on the front edge of his desk, feet crossed at the ankles, and began texting while Brass remained standing to read the report.

The foreman had stopped the job at one in the morning due to the weather and the men were sent home. There was a description of work done. Nothing besides the time was pertinent to the investigation.

Brass changed directions. "I want to talk about your mother and her two friends. They were at Delphi from around midnight to three-thirty the following morning. Did you know that?"

"I know. They've been talking about that little party for a few weeks now. I had to send some men out there to level their campsite so they wouldn't fall into the pond. Had to haul wood and set up for the campfire. You know how it is with a mother who wants something. There is no such word as 'no.' I sent some men out. Glad to do it for them." He had an easy smile.

"Did she tell you about my interview with her?"

"I heard you and your Chinese partner tried to get in Mom's house by tricking her, she asked to use the bathroom or something stupid like that. Mom said you accused her of kidnapping Warren Mitchell."

Brass didn't like Walker's flat tone. "Judging from your equipment on the job out there, you could have lowered Mitchell into that pond. The rope used to tie him is the same type as I saw on the job. The concrete he was anchored to looks like a section of curb you are putting in along Cantrell."

"Why would I do that?" Walker put his cell in his pocket and gave Brass his full attention.

"Warren Mitchell stole from your mother. That gives you motive. And you had the means and opportunity."

"Mitchell lied to her, caused her to lose money, I told Mom that was as much her fault as his. I tried to get her to divide her investment up but she was set on keeping it the way Dan had it. She is a smart woman. Sentimentality got the best of her there. Also, she isn't a poor woman, and if she needed money, I would make sure she had it. I would not jeopardize myself by kidnapping Mitchell."

"What do you know about her friends, Carol Ann Haley and Brenda Katz?"

"Mom has known them forever. We all know each other. My sisters and I went to the same grade school and high school with her kids. Brenda and Carol Ann lost money with him too and so did many other people around here."

"Who do you think has the capability of doing this to Mitchell?"

"Besides me and my mother? Dennis Moon comes to mind right away. He dates Katz. I suppose a Google search has already told you that. My dad knew him. There is an old rumor that his family has ties with the Dixie Mafia and the same goes for Jim Bud Haley. Carol Ann could have called on them. You've got some work to do to solve this puzzle."

"I am not familiar with that organization."

"It came out of Mississippi in the1960s. Only operates in the Southern states. Their specialty is moving stolen merchandise, illegal drugs, and alcohol, and retribution. Things like that.

"My dad was a Southern history buff. He said the Dixie Mafia was a loosely connected organization of violent men who'd been in prisons in the South. It isn't like *The Godfather*. Not a family. When Jim Bud Haley's plane crashed a few years back, Manny said it was the Dixie. Said that was their favorite method of assassination. They tried to assassinate Win Rockefeller that way when he was governor. Messed with the landing gear on his private plane. Just like Haley, except Rockefeller didn't die."

"Jim Bud Haley? How does he fit in to the Dixie Mafia?"

"Manny said he was the most corrupt lawyer in the state. Said he kept aged papers and inks so that he could pre-date documents and things like that. Rumored he kept files to blackmail people, that he used the Dixie Mafia to do jobs for him. Who knows? Haley was a legend around here. Bigger than life. Dad said he crossed someone. So like I said, go ahead and look into me. I don't have anything to hide." And from his open, relaxed posture, it looked to Brass like he didn't.

"Why did you sell Manny's place with all of his personal things in it?" The question came out of his subconscious. He hadn't planned on asking it when it erupted off his tongue.

"I didn't. See that warehouse over there? It is full of Manny's collections. What I left behind in that house were collectables he chose for his home. You go price one of the buffalo heads or that Indian artwork. He was proud of his place. I guess I was more sentimental than I thought when I left it in place. If doing that had kept it from selling, I would have had my men box it all up and it would be in that warehouse right now along with the rest of Dad's stuff. But you came along."

Brass didn't have a comment and turned to go.

"Brass, how'd you find the buckle?"

Brass stroked the piece of silver with his thumb. "The first time I tried to light a fire, I noticed the chimney crank was hung up on a brick that had gotten dislodged. I removed it and there it was. You hide it there?"

"Yeah, when I was a kid. I got mad at him. Dad looked for it until he died. Kept thinking it would show up. Back then, I thought it was funny, now I regret it. Manny was a sentimental man."

Brass looked down at the buckle and back at Walker. Something fleeting in his eyes told Brass that Max wasn't there. His eyes were fixed in a far-off gaze. Almost like he was asleep with his mouth slightly open. The moment passed leaving Max looking a little tired.

Brass wondered if Walker regretted that sentimental journey into the past. It revealed he was capable of strong revenge. Max used the love of an object to torture his father for over thirty years. Brass resented it for Manny. He'd lived in the house Manny built with the things the other man had collected since he'd moved to Arkansas and felt a kinship with Manny although they'd never met. Brass didn't like it that Max cheated his father out of the pleasure of the buckle. As a boy, he hid it. As a man Max should have returned it.

"Here." Brass made to remove the buckle. Max held up his hand.

"No. Buckle belongs to you now. Keep it. Just had a thought. Might help you to start stopping by the Whitewater for a beer after work. Don't take that Chinese lady with you. It's down by the capitol. Back in the old days, Clinton, Haley, Manny, the Moons, and a bunch of their buddies used to hang there. Some of them still do. Probably won't help you solve the case, but you'll get a sense of the history around here."

Chapter 12

ANNA AND MARIA
BLUE TALK THEORIES

Anna Blue was so deep into the case that she couldn't think of anything else. Maybe she was deflecting what she really wanted to think about and decided not to because the answer was not one she could get from an internet search. The implications of her mother's words, "A child nature didn't want me to have, but my husband did," sent Anna's mind thinking about her parents' relationship. She didn't want to go there, yet.

Anna laid flat on the floor to think. Yoga people call it the Corpse Pose which is a more complicated position than just lying on your back. The face has to be pointed upward at just the right angle to not cause stress on the back of the neck, the shoulders are pulled down and away from the ears, the natural arch in the lower back has to find itself. It is important not to go to sleep. For Anna, the pose allowed her body to completely relax and freed her mind so that new thoughts would come bubbling in and restore imaginative thinking.

Anna read the report from the Buffalo River accident, the reports on Haley's and Hart's plane crashes, newspaper articles about Stanford victims in the state including Hart, Haley, and Katz, personal interviews. She made a list of the victims from Arkansas and she followed up, concentrating at lot of her time on Dennis Moon, who was now on the center of her radar screen. That was the direction she needed to go, and she did, for several hours searching the net and making calls.

When you get a name, an address, and are willing to pay a few dollars for a deeper search, you get a thread, and that is all someone like Anna Blue needs to construct a picture. Several generations of the Moon family owned the kinds of businesses that are often associated with criminals because they can easily take in stolen goods and sell them. For three generations, the Moons owned pawn shops, scrap metal yards, liquor stores, and commercial real estate around Pulaski and Saline Counties. This line of inquiry led her to read about the Dixie Mafia.

Moon was dating Brenda Katz. She saw on Google Images a picture of Katz with Moon at a party given by the Arkansas Arts Center. On the website for *Soiree*, a Little Rock magazine, she found many pictures of them together. On Brenda Katz's Facebook, just the public part, she gleaned valuable information. Anna decided to brainstorm with her mother about Brenda Katz.

Maria wanted to indulge her daughter. She was relieved fate did not take Anna from her. When Anna came to her and said, "I think that Brenda Katz and her boyfriend, Dennis Moon, planned the whole thing." Maria wanted to hear Anna's thoughts.

"I know the Moon families are rich and all the young cousins go to Episcopal school, and the family contributes to all sorts of worthy causes. I think they are affiliated with the Dixie Mafia, in some way." She handed her mother a file folder.

Maria couldn't have predicted that. Anna laid out her findings and speculations in a report that impressed Maria. The depth of it all, the conclusion based on what she had found, showed the workings of her daughter's mind. It took a while for Maria to read and absorb it.

The first question Maria asked was about the line drawing Anna had done. It showed a man suspended in the water. A line around his waist was attached to an object that his feet rested on and another line ran to what looked like a dock. In the shadows stood a figure.

"What is this about?"

"Oh that. Brass described how Mitchell was tied up. And I drew it. I couldn't show in my drawing that he was wearing an old diving vest. The kind divers used a long time ago. They had to pull a cord to puncture a cartridge that would inflate the vest. That type of vest is obsolete. It was replaced by the buoyancy compensator. But Mitchell had the old style vest and it was under his shirt. Inflated. That shows he was undressed at some point and this vest was put on him. Brass thinks it was done in case he lost consciousness, someone could pull it and make him float.

"The man watching him is speculation. There was a quick release at the point where his ankles were attached to the concrete block. All a diver had to do was kick down seven feet or so. The line from his waist to the dock was needed to keep him upright. Point is, measures were in place to see that he did not drown. That means murder wasn't in the plan. Brass thinks there was a monitor, a man or maybe woman at the pond, watching to make sure he was safe."

"He didn't say anything about that earlier," Maria said.

"That's because he hadn't yet talked to the team that took Mitchell out of the water. What do you think about this idea? Katz and Moon are a couple and both are Stanford victims. Katz comes up with the idea to torture Mitchell, not kill him, just make him feel powerless like she did."

"Why do you think this was Katz's idea and not Moon's?"

"A hunch. I talked to Brass and he filled me in on the widows' reasons for being at Delphi. He said they talked about restoring themselves, purification. Water is used for purification. Baptism like they used to do in Delphi back when. Remember that preacher was drowned in Delphi. The person is dunked in water to wash away original sin. That sort of thing. I think they wanted to torture him.

"Katz had the idea to do the Samhain thing and turned her friends onto it. She wanted to be at Delphi during Mitchell's torture and needed a reason for being there. The other two didn't know about her plans."

"Mitchell was shot. How does that figure in?" Maria asked.

"That adds another dimension. I haven't figured it out yet."

"I talked to Brass. He called to check on you. Thought you should stay close to home until he gets this sorted out. You and Ron could be in danger if the person who shot Mitchell thinks you saw him."

Anna took a few minutes to absorb this news. "I would say if someone came around here looking for Ron, he would take care of it. Someone, not sure if it was a man or a woman, shot Mitchell and that means he or she knew what was going down on Delphi. You know, I just had another thought. I could substitute Haley or Hart for Katz and the theory still works. Haley or Hart could know people who would help them. I might not have this exactly right, but I am working on it. It is a possibility that all of them are guilty."

"I can't see three women agreeing on something as serious as kidnapping."

"I am just in the 'what if' stage right now. What if Brenda Katz includes her two friends on her plan for Mitchell and they go along. They decide to have

the ceremony at Delphi so they can witness it. Then one of them decides torture isn't enough and tries to shoot him. My bet is Carol Ann Haley since she
was married to Jim Bud Haley, who was thought by some to have connections
with the Dixie Mafia. Or back to my other idea; someone else unrelated to the
widows knew about their ceremony at Delphi and used them as a deflection if
something went wrong, like it did."

"Jim Bud Haley. What are you talking about? I worked with him. I have
never heard that he was a member of a mafia."

"If you get on the internet and look around at some of these conspiracy web-
sites you would come across the Dixie. It is not an official organization, like a
crime family. It's not something Haley would join. It's more like he knew some
of the people associated with it and used them to do things for him. I will give
you the link where you can read about Haley's accident."

"Sites like that are gossip and speculation."

"Mom! Reality and fantasy tend to play together. Think outside the box. I
might not be right but I am onto something, I feel it."

Chapter 13

✳   ✳   ✳

FRIENDSHIP

Carol Ann sat in her mother's Prius outside of Isabelle Hart's house with her little dog Jazzy Marie, thinking about what she was about to do. Her mother died the year before and Carol Ann kept the car and the title and registration in her mother's name. She felt anonymous when she drove it.

Isabelle was at the police station with Brass and Carol Ann hoped to get her work done before she got back. She knew the code to the back gate that guarded the road that ran around the far end of the property to Isabelle's greenhouse and boat dock. Carol Ann punched the numbers in, the gate slid back, she pulled in and drove to the dock. She unloaded the contents of the Whole Foods bags and cardboard boxes that contained shredded documents, cellphones, thumb drives, laptops, hand guns, and other secret items into the boat.

Carol Ann didn't want to involve Isabelle. She needed her boat to make sure these things disappeared forever. She started the engine, Jazzy sat in her lap, and they headed upriver. When she got to a place she felt safe about, she began dropping the items one by one into the water as she steered staying in what she figured was the deepest and swiftest part of the current. She prayed she would finish and get back to her home before Isabelle returned, but she didn't.

As Carol Ann pulled onto Penal Farm Road, she saw Isabelle's car coming toward her and stopped and rolled down her window.

"I was looking for you," Carol Ann said. "Sorry I didn't call first. I just now remembered where you were off to this morning." Before she could say more, Isabelle interrupted.

"Turn around. I want to talk. Brass said Mitchell was shot."

Carol Ann followed Isabelle back to the house and they parked next to the greenhouse.

"What are you doing with Thor?"

"I took him with me. He had to go to the vet for his nail trim and I didn't have time to come back here and get him."

"What did Brass think about that?"

"No comment and his cheeky partner wasn't there." She removed the bird's travel cage from her BMW station wagon and took it into the greenhouse, opened the door, and let Thor free to soar above several varieties of exotic orchids and edible mushrooms, including one type of mushroom commonly called magic. Five laps around the twenty-five yard long building satisfied the parrot and he landed on Isabelle's shoulder. Brenda carried Jazzy and the four of them walked out into the enclosed breezeway that connected the greenhouse to the garage which connected to the house.

"I came out here to ask if I could use your boat. I wanted to get rid of the gun. You weren't here so I took it. I hope you don't mind. I was afraid they would get a warrant and search my house."

Isabelle said, "I think they are going to search all of our houses looking for that gun and whatever else they can find. Brass asked me if he could pick up my robe so they could check it for gunshot residue and rule me out. I gave him the Shin's ticket. He wanted to know why I was so quick to have it cleaned. I asked him what he would do with a pair of jeans he was wearing while he sat on the ground around a pond where ducks shit all the time. Would he just hang them in his closet? Where is yours?"

"I dropped it off at Shin's too, except I washed it first to be sure. I guess they will have to settle for Brenda's, if they can find it down in her laundry room."

Carol Ann and Isabelle entered the garage and took the service elevator up and walked out into the butler's pantry and then into the kitchen. The parrot flew through the kitchen into its aviary, climbed up to the highest perch, then started calling the dog's name and barking.

"What were you thinking when you brought that gun? I know why you said you fired it. The mystery man, right? Now, it seems you are either a really bad shot or you knew more about what was going on at Delphi than you told us."

"I never feel safe if I'm not armed. You know that. I didn't tell you and Brenda since you were so into doing the ceremony just like Laurel Moon said. I had to make a judgement call. It was between me feeling safe or you and Brenda following her instructions. That other man had a gun. I swear he did. I shot in his direction to scare him away."

"I get that. So why not tell the police?"

"Well, if I did they would want to see my gun and test it and all. And then they might find it had been used in an unsolved crime back a while ago. Now it isn't an issue."

"You are going to have to be a little more clear, Carol Ann. Those detectives know we are hiding something. We are suspicious because of what we don't say not what we do. They can feel there is something off with us."

"It is not that simple, really. Remember when Oliver Robertson was found shot in the park across from the Peabody hotel, well it wasn't called that back then, what was the name? I can't remember."

"The Excelsior."

"Jim Bud did it, accidentally, of course. He got Oliver help right away and left the scene before anyone saw him. Point is, they might be able to connect my gun to that case." It wasn't exactly the truth but close enough.

"I thought you didn't want to tell the cops because you didn't have a permit or a registration. Now we know there was a crime. Warren cheated us out of millions. That's motive and we were at the crime scene. All he needs is means. You know that."

"We are not his only victims. It's not a crime to be present at a scene where one is committed. If we did find someone to do it for us, why would we be out at Delphi? Only fools would do that. Besides, it is a stretch of the imagination to think we could physically do the thing. Get a grip. Brass is fishing.

"I told you already, I was shooting at the man who was following us. I didn't shoot Mitchell. I didn't even know he was there. How could I? Maybe the mystery man was using Mitchell as target practice, like he was a turtle—god knows he deserved it, that bastard."

"Hold on, Carol Ann. I thought you'd forgiven Warren, now you are saying he deserved it. Never mind, go back to the gun and Jim Bud. Explain all of that."

"Well, remember it was all over the papers. Oliver Robertson was an architect and someone shot him and it was never solved. I am saying that it was Jim Bud who did it with the gun I had the other night. So the gun had to disappear."

"How did Jim Bud accidentally shoot him?"

"Oh, I don't know. It happened." Carol Ann felt something inside of her snap. She was tired down to her bone marrow and had not slept. She suddenly stood up and shouted, "If you are determined to bring Jim Bud into this whole thing and turn me in as the person who fired a shot, and if you want to tell the police that I told you and Brenda to lie, go ahead. You do what you need to feel safe. Because you are not safe. Safety is an illusion." With that she picked up Jazzy Marie and left Isabelle sitting there alone in her house with her talking parrot.

Carol Ann walked out of the front door, hurried down the spiral stairs, across the bridge, and ran to her mother's Prius. The tires threw gravel as she spun around and charged out through the gate. It was a good thing it was open or she would have smashed it to pieces. She rolled down her window, took her revolver out of her purse, and shot it six times into the air. It was the same gun she'd played the spin game with the night before except this morning it was fully loaded. Last night reminded her that her time wasn't up; yet, she was getting a little tired of this life without Jim Bud. More and more she felt there was nothing left to keep her here on this earth. A woman with nothing to lose can be a dangerous animal.

Isabelle heard the shots. Carol Ann was having a meltdown. She was sorry she had pushed her so hard, yet it didn't feel hard. Of the three of them, Carol Ann was more attached to her husband then either she or Brenda were to theirs. They felt freedom when their husbands died; Carol Ann felt true loss. Isabelle went to the aviary and got Thor. He stepped up on her arm and together they watched the river as it flowed past their house.

Isabelle thought about Oliver Robertson. She was so shocked by Carol Ann's revelation, that is sparked something inside of her and she felt there were lies sprinkled in. She remembered it was front page news for a while and there was much speculation about who did it. Was it a crime organization or a jealous lover? Robertson was found behind the stairwell on the river side of the elevated sidewalk that connected the Excelsior to the river park on the other side of the busy street. The park was a favorite place for bums to hang around at night and office workers to eat their lunches on pretty days. The back of the red brick stairwell was the only place a person on the park trail could not be seen from the road, or the hotel, or the old State House.

The newspapers said that a bartender at the bar and grill at the Excelsior saw a woman cross over the bridge around two in the afternoon. A few minutes later he saw Robertson, a man he recognized as a good customer, cross over. He said that neither Robertson nor the woman appeared on the trail. He said he figured they were behind the stairwell and didn't think anything about it until the ambulance and police cars came.

Isabelle went back through her old calendars to see what she was doing on that day. She was at an orchid growers' seminar and Dan was down in Stuttgart duck hunting with Jim Bud. She couldn't think of why Carol Ann would lie. Her friend was a complex woman. More than once, she wondered what that consistently happy face was hiding.

Carol Ann was disappointed in herself. As it turned out, the lie didn't need to be told at all. She had feared the bullet lodged in the body she had shot, but it hadn't. In the old days, she would have reacted differently. She would have let it play out a little longer and been patient. The problem, if it turned out there was one, could have been solved without asking her friends to lie. She used to be so calm, didn't blurt out stupid stuff when she was frightened. All that had changed with Jim Bud's death. He steadied her and now she fully realized how she needed that anchor.

Carol Ann thought about that day. Robertson wasn't supposed to die. Who would have known he had a blood-clotting disorder. If he had not been an abuser, he might still be alive.

Carol Ann remembered the first time she met him. It was right after Robertson signed the contact to design the Excelsior. She went with Haley to the celebration party. A handsome man, tall, charismatic, with something mean in his eyes as he appraised every young woman in the room. Carol Ann watched him work the guests and put herself in his path. He didn't seem interested in conversation with her, she was a little old for him, until he learned whose wife she was, and then, he was locked in.

Not long after, a friend brought a woman to the Twenty-Eight Hundred Club who looked fresh out of graduate school. Carol Ann's daughter Melissa would have been about the same age, if she had not been killed by a drunk driver the night of her high school graduation. Carol Ann liked Jeanne immediately and a friendship started between them. If her son had not been gay, Carol Ann thought Jeanne would have made her the perfect daughter-in-law.

Jeanne worked for the Robertson firm. She began stopping by The Club regularly. It didn't take long for Carol Ann to notice the signs. Jeanne was in a relationship with an abuser. As time passed and trust developed, Carol Ann learned Jeanne was involved with her boss, Oliver Robertson. And she was not surprised to learn that Jeanne's father had been a hitter. Carol Ann told Jeanne about her first husband and how that ended. She offered her a place to stay so she would not have to pay rent if she lost her job when she walked away from the affair with her boss.

Jeanne got the courage to break it off and showed up at Carol Ann's door at one in the morning with her front tooth in her hand and a growing bruise on the side of her head. She refused to go to the emergency room, just wanted a place to sleep, and Carol Ann gave it to her. The next morning Carol Ann took her to the dentist. The morning after, Jeanne said she was leaving Little Rock, that Robertson found her a job in Texas, and showed her a cashier's check for the total amount she owed in student loans.

Jeanne promised Carol Ann she was going to get therapy and Carol Ann hoped that she would. That was three years before Oliver Robertson was found behind the stairwell dead with part of his dick blown off. Carol Ann hadn't intended to shoot him, just scare him. She had learned Oliver was abusing a young woman from his office as he had Jeanne. It pissed her off when she saw Oliver at the candlelight vigil on the University of Arkansas campus remembering the Little Rock victims of domestic violence.

The Chief of Police, Marshall Knight, with a survivor at his side, read the names of one hundred ten women killed by domestic violence. It was heart-wrenching for Carol Ann to hear the names of these women and to see Oliver standing next to the chief. Robertson was introduced to the crowd as a generous contributor to the nonprofit Arkansans Against Domestic Violence. It was then that she swore to do something about Oliver Robertson

Carol Ann had planned to toss the gun in the river as soon as she'd shot him; instead, she kept it. Her biggest fear was Jim Bud would find out, but he didn't. She hadn't planned on bringing the gun to the Samhain ceremony. At the last minute she changed her mind and decided she would to toss it into Delphi to symbolize that she was shedding herself of the parts of her past she regretted, and she did regret Oliver's death. A long life without his penis and a bag to catch his urine was what he deserved, but she had miscalculated.

This trip into the past caused her to miss the driveway to her house and she had to turn around at the next street. That was when she noticed a brown Ford with black rims in her drive. It had to be a cop car so she kept on going until she reached the Sam's Club. A bit of shopping at the warehouse would calm her nerves. Maybe her breakdown at Isabelle's and remembering Oliver was a good thing. It focused her mind and reminded her that she had done nothing wrong at Delphi, and that was what counted.

Chapter 14

DETECTIVE CALASA

Trudi Calasa drove back to Carol Ann Haley's house. If the woman had gone for a walk with her dog, she should be home by now. Trudi rang the bell. Banged on the door. She knocked on every window she could reach and walked around the house again and again, looking for signs of anything that would give her cause to enter the house. The problem was the alarm system. When she looked through the living room window she could see the front door and the alarm panel. It was armed. If someone had broken in, it would have gone off already so that excuse wouldn't work.

Trudi phoned Isabelle Hart and asked if she could have a word about Carol Ann, who seemed to be missing. Isabelle was expecting it. Brenda had gotten the same kind of call a couple of hours earlier.

Trudi explained she had been at the house and was worried that there was still no response either to her phone calls or her knocking. "Do you think she could be inside of the house in need of assistance? Maybe she has fallen or had a heart attack."

Isabelle decided to take a different attitude toward the detective and be a little more forthcoming with information, play nice. "Carol Ann was just here a while ago. She and Jazzy Marie had been walking the loop at Two Rivers. That's close to my house and they stopped by. I think she had shopping to do. I'm not sure where. Wait. I'll text her."

Trudi waited for several minutes.

"Carol Ann's at Sam's. She'll be home in an hour or so. I told her you were worried about her."

"Her car is here." There was only one car registered to Haley and that was the green Jaguar sitting in the drive. "Is she with someone?"

"I don't know about that. She wasn't with anyone when she was here." Isabelle did not say Carol Ann was in her mother's Prius.

"I tried her cell. Maybe I have the wrong number." She gave Isabelle the number she had been calling.

"That's the right one. Carol Ann has different ringtones for people like me, Brenda, her son. You know. If she doesn't recognize the tone, she will let it go to voicemail, and she doesn't always check that regularly."

Trudi wondered why the woman was being civil to her and that made her wonder if she had something to hide, but she'd been wondering that all along.

She called Brass. "I'm still out in front of Haley's. Have you gotten a warrant?"

"You know we don't have enough. So get her robe."

"Thanks, Brass," she said to dead air.

Carol Ann called Isabelle a few minutes later, apologized, and thanked her for the heads-up.

Isabelle said, "I've been thinking and you are right about no mention of the gun. Why muddy the water? About Jim Bud, that is none of my business. He was a good man." Then Isabelle and Carol Ann said at the same time, "And a good man is hard to find," and laughed. The rough patch between them was over.

Carol Ann placed a call to her hairdresser. "Bobby, I believe you told me your car was in the shop and you were getting rides from friends. How about I stop by and you run me home. Then you can use my extra car until yours is ready."

Bobby was pleased and Carol Ann was more pleased when the shampoo girl drove back with her instead of Bobby. He was a little nosey and gossipy and would probably recognize an unmarked police car since he had done a little bit of time for child porn or something slimy like that. She appreciated his talent with hair and Bobby didn't know that she knew about his past.

Trudi was looking down at her cell when a white car pulled into the drive. Carol Ann got out and a young woman helped her unload her supplies from Sam's. There wasn't a tag on the front and the car backed out of the drive. Trudi couldn't get the plate numbers.

"Well, I'll be, my personal protector. I heard you were worried I was laid out dead in my house." She gave Trudi a wink and indicated the sacks. "Would you mind. My back is a little tired." Jazzy Marie jumped up and down against Trudi's leg.

"I saw your car and thought you were home."

Haley didn't act like she heard and kept walking toward the kitchen.

"Isabelle Hart said you were out at her place. She didn't mention anyone was with you."

"It was just me and Jazzy." Carol Ann knew the detective wanted to know who the white car belonged to and who was driving it. She would have to ask outright. Less said the better.

"I am starving," Carol Ann said as she sat down the bags, opened her desk drawer, took out a handful of menus, and selected one from the Saigon Cafe. "I would like soup with coconut milk in it and some fried rice. Here, let me know what you want. They deliver."

Trudi looked it over and decided not to take Carol Ann up on her offer even though she would have liked some fried spring rolls and an order of green papaya salad.

"Okay then. I'll just place my order and we can get down to the reasons you're here." She smiled at Trudi as she dialed the memorized number. When she got off the phone, Trudi commented, "It sounds like they know you. You eat there a lot?"

"I eat Saigon's food often. I have it delivered. I got into the habit of having meals at home after Jim Bud died. Just wasn't up to going to all of the places we went. And now I find it is my preferred way."

Trudi got down to the reason she had been waiting half of the day to talk with Haley. "We need to eliminate you as the person who discharged the firearm. To do that, I need the robe you were wearing. I have an evidence bag with me. Would you get it for me?"

"Honey, I would be glad to except I sent that filthy thing to the cleaners. Didn't even bring it past the front door. It smelled like duck shit and who knows what else. We should have brought something to sit on. Here." She handed Trudi a ticket from Shin's Cleaners. "Just pick it up. Mr. Shin will put it on my account."

Trudi took the stub knowing the evidence was gone. She hoped Katz's robe showed something useful.

"Why did you keep Mitchell as your investment advisor after what happened?"

"Trudi, people make mistakes, especially those under pressure for a long time. Warren worked hard, and he had heavy expenses especially after his wife came down with cancer. That was extremely expensive for him. When I met Warren, he and three or four of his friends worked for Merrill and then they went to Stillpoint Management and that company was bought out by Stanford.

"Warren didn't do his homework on Stanford. He just went along with the others.This whole business has pretty much ruined his credibility but he has stuck in there and is starting to recover. Mostly, though, I stayed because of his wife; we are friends, she comes by The Club sometimes. She was here quite a bit when she first got diagnosed. We have a number of Pink Ribbon women who stop by."

"Pink Ribbon?"

"Cancer survivors. My mother was a survivor. She's gone now, was over ninety when she passed. Survivors stick together. I have heard the people who invested in Stanford CDs described as victims. I don't think of myself that way. I have survived the loss. Yes, I have had to scale back my lifestyle, but I still have a pretty good one."

"Isabelle Hart doesn't feel that way. She didn't stick with Mitchell. Did that cause any friction between you two?"

"What are you talking about, friction? I did split my portfolio in half to diversify. I wasn't sure how Warren would emotionally recover and I wanted to show support but not put my whole financial future on the line. Brenda is an accountant and she never had all of her investments with him. Isabelle's split with Warren completely and she's wised up and has diversified her investments. Have you ever been married, Trudi?"

"No, ma'am."

"If the man is the main breadwinner or handles most of the finances, and he passes away, the widow tends to follow the financial path he put them on. Widows rarely strike out in a different direction. Brenda is a money person. She kept a good amount with Warren because her husband trusted him. One of his partners advised Brenda to quit doing business with Warren when he went with Stanford yet she still kept some investments with him."

Carol Ann sounded sincere and open and she looked like it too. Trudi decided it was time to shake her up. "You know that you and your friends are our primary suspects. All of you have the same motive. The fact that you and Isabelle Hart were so quick to take the robes you wore to the cleaners is suspicious. It would relieve some of that if you would give my team permission to search your home without a warrant."

Carol Ann weighed the pros and cons. She knew they did not have the evidence it would take to get a judge to agree to a warrant to search her house. If she had not been to the river that morning, she would have refused the offer.

"Just you go ahead and look in every nook and cranny. Get all your police friends in here to help you. Now, don't tear my home to pieces like they do on those crime shows. Leave it like you found it. I don't want to see my thong panties strung across my bedroom floor, if you get my meaning."

Carol Ann had the happy face down to an art and it was now the mask on her face. She learned it young, from her mother, who was married to a hitter. *Put a big smile on your face and hide your troubles. No one wants to hear about them anyway.* Those were her mother's words of wisdom and Carol Ann took them to heart. It was a lucky day for all of them when her dad died.

The doorbell rang and Jazzy Marie expressed her displeasure. Carol Ann gave the driver a tip and turned to Trudi. "I am going to take my lunch and go into my den and have a martini and enjoy my meal. You do whatever it is you need to do."

Trudi made a call to Brass and began her search in Haley's bedroom. The others would arrive soon and they would go through this big house with all of its Oriental vases, antique boxes, blown-glass collections, miniature sculptures, and every other item that looked to Trudi like a dust collector. Haley wasn't a hoarder though. Her house was tastefully decorated with everything imaginable. There was a lot to go through and her team would do it thoroughly.

Carol Ann sat down in her rocker with a cucumber-infused martini. She texted Hart and copied Katz. Figuring Brass would take a look at her cell sooner or later, she typed her message with that in mind. *The cops are tearing up my house from stem to stern looking for that gun they asked about. I hope Jim Bud is up there looking down on these poor fools. Come by at five.* The warning was really for Isabelle.

Chapter 15

RICHARD BLUE

A nna noticed her dad's open laptop on his desk as she walked past his home
office. Richard usually closed it down and put it away in the middle desk
drawer before he left for work. Maria, gone to exercise classes at the athletic
club, wouldn't be back for a couple of hours. Anna didn't hesitate or feel a smidgen of guilt over invading her father's privacy. She sat down. She had plenty of
time and settled in to see what she could find.

Anna could have opened the laptop anytime she wanted, the code never
changed, it was one-four-three and a dollar sign. She'd figured it out when
she was thirteen. One- four-three meant "I love you" in their personal family
code. When they hung up from a phone call when others were around, they
would say "goodbye one-four-three" to each other. Back when she was trying
to work out how to get into his computer, she put in the numbers and followed
it with "AnnaMaria," and it didn't work. She tried a few variations, then she
thought, *What does he love as much as us?* That was money. The word "money"
didn't work—the dollar sign did.

Anna told herself she would never open the laptop using the password unless her dad left it on and open to the world, that was fair game. She also knew
and did not use all of his passwords to his documents and his email. He wrote

them out on a note card, taped it to the underside of his desk drawer, and looked at the card using a little mirror. His habit was to change them every six weeks. Her dad was so unoriginal and predictable.

She ran her finger across the pad and the screen came to page thirteen in the middle of what looked like a trust document. Her father specialized in contract law and she wondered if this was his personal trust so she went to the beginning. She scrolled through the pages: it looked boring, until she came to the trustee's responsibilities regarding the grantor's widow and children.

When the trust went into effect her father would become trustee and re-sponsible for a long list of things including inspecting the widow's house in which she and her two children lived. He was to evaluate its cleanliness, hoard-ing, maintenance, and so on, and he, or a representative, was to do these in-spections quarterly. Her father was to hire a private detective to investigate the friends of this man's children, his widow's friends, neighbors, after-school activities, who spent the night at the house, where they vacationed and with whom, and on and on for pages. There were as many rules for his wife as he had for his kids.

The widow had no control over the money left in a trust for her. Anna's dad was responsible for paying all of the bills for the household, for vacations, schooling, and so on. The widow got a monthly allowance and a yearly bonus if she obeyed the rules. Her father would become this woman's financial husband, more of one than Warren Mitchell was to his widowed clients. All Mitchell did was manage their brokerage accounts—and still he'd managed to screw it up. Her father would have the responsibilities of a husband for a woman he wasn't married to and a father, of sorts, more a protector, to the kids. Anna wondered if her mother knew.

Anna Blue could not imagine her father creating such a document to control her mother's life after he died. Either this man's wife was a half-wit who could not handle a household alone or she was being punished from beyond the grave by an insanely controlling husband. It seemed to her there was a resentment and revenge in the trust but what did she know about marriages, or even relationships. She'd never had a boyfriend. Anna went back to the beginning of the document and read it again and then started going over it one more time.

Anna was deep into it and didn't hear her mother pull up in the drive. Some sort of sixth sense alerted her. She closed the laptop and left her dad's office before her mother opened the front door and called her name. Her father, when this man died, would have a second family. Or maybe the man was already dead. That was easy enough to find out and Anna would as soon as she had the chance. Dead? Could that be why her father seemed remote and distracted the past several weeks?

Maybe he was having an affair with this man's widow, Anna thought, and then wondered why she'd wondered that. Anna asked herself why would he take on such a long-term and intricate responsibility and then she chided herself. His password said it all, one–four–three–dollar sign. The man must be a multimillionaire and the trustee compensation plus the money coming into her dad's firm for the legal and accounting fees his associates would charge to help the trustee administer the various parts of the trust would be worth hundreds of thousands a year. It was about money. Of course.

All Anna could think about was finding out all she could about this client who was determined to control his money, his widow, and his children after he died, and had hired her father to make it happen. She thought maybe the man didn't trust her father because he had set up a trust protector to oversee her father's actions. She bet her dad didn't like that one bit. All of Richard's associates were young lawyers, women except for one man, all graduated with honors from Bowen law school where he had studied law. She needed time to think and her mom was coming in the house.

"Hi, Moma." Anna stood in the kitchen making popcorn, old style, in the iron Dutch oven over the flame of the gas stove. "Have a good workout?"

"Smells like comfort food to me. How are you doing?" Marie said as she hugged her daughter and stepped back and looked at her. "What are you up to?"

"Popcorn."

"Don't think so." Marie had a knack for seeing beneath the surface. And for a minute, or less, Anna thought about evading her mother's instinctual question but decided to go with the truth.

"Dad left his computer on. I looked at the open document. Do you know Dad is or is going to become a financial husband to some woman who has two little kids when the guy dies or maybe he is already dead?"

Maria Blue stood there in her yoga togs and seemed to freeze in place in front of her daughter. "What's going on?"

Anna told what she knew. Maria didn't comment.

"Finish the corn, get the laptop, and meet me on the deck. Too pretty a day to spend inside. I need a shower." What Maria needed was time to think. She knew this trust, had seen it before, parts of it, the names of the individuals involved were redacted from her copy. Around the time McCoy was closing down his active practice and getting ready to buy a horse farm in Fayetteville, he'd given her the job of creating a psychological profile of the trust's owner based solely on the document. That was one of the more unusual requests that he'd made of her over the years. The document made a deep impression on Maria and she had thought about it several times since.

As Maria turned on the four shower-heads that surrounded her circular shower stall, and waited for the water to heat, she remembered wondering who would take on the job of trustee for this estate. It would mean an immersion into the lives of the widow and the children if the trust was activated before the children reached twenty-one.

The widow would never have control over her financial life if her total support came from the trust. Now she wondered if McCoy had redacted the names or if the document had come to him that way. When he'd asked for her analysis, she hadn't asked him, she just assumed it had arrived that way. McCoy told her another attorney had hired him to find the flaws, play devil's advocate, and he wanted to understand the grantor.

Maria remembered trying to imagine how she would feel if Richard died and left these instructions, rather restrictions, for her life. That was easy, angry. The first thing she would do was try to get the evil thing broken. The trustee would be taking on a second family. How would that affect the trustee's personal life? How could it not, if he carried out the rules as written? The trustee had an enormous amount of discretion, he could choose to let the slimier things slide and not get into the nitty gritty personal life of the family.

She remembered thinking, she was glad Richard's practice focused on contract law and not trusts. The word "trust" meant control, family feuds, lawsuits. Why didn't people just give to a person outright? Make a simple will, pay the taxes, go on. Without trusts, though, attorneys like McCoy wouldn't have thriving practices making, breaking, and defending them.

Marie stood under the pounding hot water and said to herself, "Today is a day I am always going to remember." She felt betrayed by McCoy and her husband, knowing that was not fair to them but feeling it anyway. They were holding true to confidentiality, that was their job: she was not a part of it, yet she was.

Now, she understood why McCoy asked her to do the profile on the mystery man. It was his way of letting her know, hoping she would guess, without breaking the lawyer-client confidentiality code. He probably thought she would find a clue as to who the client was and figure out the trustee. But Maria had focused on the parts of the document that gave her an understanding of the grantor. If she had strayed and looked at other sections, she might have realized it was Richard.

"Moma," Anna called from the door of the shower room, "Dad called. I didn't pick up, just wanted you to know. I'll be out on the deck."

Maria had noticed a change in her husband lately, but, unlike Anna, she wouldn't dig into his business. Richard didn't talk about his work with her, never had, and she accepted that without liking it. She was smart, lawyers consulted her for picking jurors, and for her psychological insights into their clients. She was good at being a jury consultant, the best in Arkansas, yet her husband never asked what she thought about anything concerning his work. There were times when she wondered if he trusted her or if he was paranoid or maybe it was his military training even though he wasn't in special forces or anything.

Maybe it was because she wasn't his first choice as a wife. Maria knew Richard's mother had favored her as a daughter-in-law when he had someone else in mind, and Richard was all about pleasing his mother. From the choice of his professions, lawyer and accountant, to the suits he wore and the car he drove, his mother's opinion was important to him. Maria married Richard because she had always been crazy about him. They'd been friends since junior high, hung around together, and seemed to fit with each other. Maria thought they were meant to be together—maybe now he regretted it.

Marie looked at her trim body in the mirror as she dried off. She let the white oversized towel fall and her hands hesitated over her lower abdomen where her ovaries were located. The ones she'd thought didn't work right but in the end found out the fertility problems didn't belong to her. Specialists in infertility should have looked at Richard's slow swimmers before pumping her full of hormones. The fertility issue still stung between them, that was evident from her rant and remark about a child nature didn't want her to have. Maybe nature was protecting her in ways she hadn't wanted to think about. "Don't go there," she said out loud to herself.

Anna was sitting on the deck, her feet on the rail, a red bowl of popcorn on her lap. The laptop was closed on the table. A blue bowl sat next to it and a beer.

"What's this?" Maria smiled as she picked up the cold beer and chugged it down and let out a long, loud, juicy burp and said, "That's more like it."

"Thought you might need a recovery drink after that workout. That was one of your best burps. I'll give it a nine."

Chapter 16

Max Walker's Ordeal

The morning Anna Blue was invading her father's privacy, Max Walker was on his way to Pinnacle Mountain to meet four of his cycling buddies. He wasn't feeling himself.

He figured it was a hangover from his fiftieth birthday party the night before. He drank a little too much beer and wondered if he alone had consumed the whole keg. When he got to Penal Farm Road, he took a right, instead of going straight down Highway 10 to meet his friends.

Was it a coincidence that the road he took led to his mother's house? As he turned the wheel of the Denali, his right eye seemed to drift in that direction and stay there as the center of his right-side vision turned into a spot so muddy that he could barely see through it. He had a family history of glaucoma in the right eye. Hadn't he just seen the eye doctor and been declared perfect? He couldn't remember.

All he could think of was he needed to see Moma. He heard his horn honking itself and realized he'd stopped the car. Picking up his cell, his fingers couldn't find the right keys to punch. He started giggling and it wasn't funny.

Then it seemed that magically the car door opened and he felt his mother's familiar touch on his shoulder.

"Moma. I can't see right. There is a brown spot. I'm off in my body. Feel dizzy."

Isabelle took his hand in hers and used the other to call 911. As she spoke to the operator, she pulled Max across the seat and got behind the wheel, deciding that it would be quicker to drive him to the hospital than wait for an ambulance. The next call she made was to Richard Blue.

"I'm taking Max to emergency at St. Vincent. It doesn't look good. I think he's having a stroke."

"I'm okay now," she heard Max say as they turned on to the interstate. He didn't seem to be talking to anyone in particular. "I'm okay. Probably shouldn't have taken the Benadryl with the sleeping pill after all that beer. I'm seeing better too, not so much brown."

"So you want me to take you back to my house?"

"Yeah."

"You had a stroke." She started not to say it. Knowing Max, if he was feeling up to it, he would argue and she wanted to shut that down before he could get started.

"No, I didn't. I can talk. I can smile, see," and he could, but that didn't matter to Isabelle; she kept on speeding because he didn't look right to her.

"You've been saying for a long time you haven't felt right in your body. Now you can get it checked out." He wasn't listening. His eyes were fixed, rigid, and she wondered if he was having a seizure. She'd seen that lately, the eyes fixed, hardness passing across his face, and wondered if he had developed epilepsy or something or maybe it was the cancer treatments making him tired. She'd drawn it to his attention a few weeks ago, and he cut her off so she left it alone. Now she could see what she'd noticed was important. Maybe if she'd pursued it, he wouldn't be in this condition.

Richard arrived at emergency reception before she did and he filled out the paperwork. Isabelle went into the exam room with Max. She called Carley but didn't expect her to pick up early on a Saturday morning. She texted her—no reply. Two hours after arriving and after some preliminary testing, the doctor recommended an MRI of Max's brain.

While the test was going on, Carley rushed through the double doors looking like she was ready to go for a workout at Little Rock Country Club, dressed in her usual tight stretchy pants, running shoes, a fitted tank top. Her ten-year-old daughter said it perfectly when Isabelle overheard her describing her mother to one of her school friends. "She always wears exercise outfits but she never exercises."

Because she had a rather long torso for a person five feet tall, combined with short legs and arms, and a head a little larger than normal and made to look bigger by a mass of long, dyed-blond hair, Carley would have been a dachshund if she were a dog. That might be the reason the weenie dog was her favorite breed. She'd gotten her first one from her father for her eighth birthday and as one dog passed it was always replaced with another puppy that would grow up to look just like the one before it.

Isabelle's personal name for her daughter-in-law was "Lollipop." Carley always dressed like a teenager. In spite of the Botox and nips and tucks, up close she looked her forty-four years. As Carly walked toward her, Isabelle focused on her son's wife. She was a caricature of how she wanted others to see her. Isabelle coached herself, "Be nice to her."

As Isabelle explained to Carley what had happened, Carley flipped a chunk of hair between her neck and ear with her left index and middle fingers. If habitual hair stroking is a way to comfort oneself, then Carley was in constant need of soothing. Since stroking was her comfort tool then her escape tool was the cellphone Carley always seemed to have in her hand. She could barely keep her eyes off the screen, checking for messages, or using it as a recording device, or a camera. Texting was her main iPhone activity.

Carley spoke in a low voice. "I don't like it here. These people don't know what they are doing. I'm calling a friend and getting him into UAMS. The mother of one of the girls in Cici's dance classes has a friend whose husband is a surgeon or something there. He's a big deal. This is bullshit. They should know what is wrong by now."

"In hospital time, this probably is normal. St. Vincent is a good spot until they find out what's going on," Isabelle said but Carly wasn't listening. She was poking a number into her phone.

"Well, we'll see." She turned her back to Isabelle and spoke into her cell, "Erin. Hi. It's Carley. I need a favor."

After another hour or so, a physician came out, introduced himself, and spoke with Isabelle, Richard, and Carley.

"The MRI shows multiple hemorrhagic infarcts on his brain and—"

Carley interrupted him. "How do you spell that?" She had her phone out, ready to consult Google.

The physician clarified, blood clots, and Carley again demanded a spelling of the unfamiliar word so he gave it to her.

Isabelle stepped forward and introduced herself as the patient's mother and the physician directed his analysis to her as Carley consulted the internet.

The doctor recommended admission and a thorough workup with various specialists. As he was making his recommendation, Carley interrupted. "You can stop there. We aren't staying. I am taking him to the UAMS hospital. So forget it."

"That's not your decision to make. The patient is awake and fully capable of making his own health care decisions."

"We will see about that. I have a friend at UAMS. He will take care of it. Now do what you need to do to get him moved over there." The physician informed Carley that he would consult with his patient which he did.

Although Isabelle had her son's health care proxy, he was still able to make his own decisions. It was up to him to move to another hospital or not and he decided that was what he would do. Round one to Carley.

The physician discharged him against medical advice to UAMS hospital where further workups would reveal a pulmonary vein thrombus. Upon this diagnosis, and because there was not a cardiac surgeon at UAMS who would attempt the surgery, which held a high risk of death or a massive stroke, Max was readmitted to Saint Vincent. It was noted in his chart that he showed significant neurological decline since his initial admission to their emergency room. Here was another family drama to add to the list.

Chapter 17

LAUREL MOON

Kristin met Brass for a late lunch at Brave New Restaurant. It was located in an office park that had at one time been the River Dale Country Club. The view of the Arkansas River was great and the food superb at Brave New. It was Kristin's pick. His hangout, the Red Door, was just a few blocks away.

Brass ordered beer with the seafood special and Kristin a glass of Pinot Grigio and the pasta salad, then she filled him in on the facts about Laurel Moon.

"The name on her birth certificate is Betty Jo Moon and she was born in Fort Smith. There is still a branch of the Moon family up there. She went to nursing school and came out with a degree in practical nursing, not a registered nurse. She opened up her own business helping people with terminal illnesses die and she also did house and dog sitting. She had four women working for her.

"Moon was stealing from her clients and was caught selling stolen merchandise. That bought her eighteen months at McPherson. I wonder if that's where she learned to commune with the spirits. Anyway, after she got out of prison, Laurel, aka Betty Jo, went into the psychic business.

"She must have some sort of insight into crime since she has helped the police solve a few crimes, according to her website and some newspaper articles. I'm not saying her insight was otherworldly. It was probably just a matter of connections.

"The Moon family walks a thin line between legal and illegal with all of their business interests. Plus, it is hard to separate rumor from fact about them. Mitchell introduced Dennis Moon and Brenda Katz and they are tight. He is a dumpy little man and not at all like her handsome husband that got whacked by a tree limb. Yet they are definitely a couple.

"Anyway, Dennis is what I will call the boss of the family businesses and she does consulting work for them. I've followed rumors about the family's supposed involvement with the Dixie Mafia but can't substantiate anything. Dennis Moon and Jim Bud Haley were friends, plus Moon and Mitchell also go back some years."

"The whole thing sounds incestuous," Brass said. "After all, this is the South."

"Dennis Moon has the connections to extract any form of revenge he wants on anyone around here. He is definitely worth looking at. Also, Walker, the man whose house you bought, was tight friends with Moon. If the Moons needed a lot paved, Manny did it. If they needed someone to clear out a tenant from one of their buildings, Walker sent his guys in at night and cleaned the place out. Moon and Walker were regulars at the Whitewater.

"Mitchell's water torture in Delphi is right down the alley of the Dixie Mafia. Although there isn't proof, some say they turned on Jim Bud Haley and took him down.

"One more thing. I took a side trip, after you told me about the new client who came to see Mitchell the night he was kidnapped. Thanks to your man, Tim, I got the records on all the unsolved crimes in the past fifteen years that involved an unidentified woman, a gunshot wound, and either murder or torture. Guess who popped up on that list? Oliver Robertson. You were not living here back then. It was a really big deal. Here is that file and a couple of others. The reason Robertson stands out to me is he was a client of Jim Bud Haley. This whole case looks like a spider web of connections."

"That's quite a report." He didn't know how it would help the case but it would help the new script he was working on. "Trudi is searching Haley's house, looking for guns and anything else that can point to her or her friends. Haley agreed to the search without a warrant."

"That's a waste of time. If Trudi finds anything, I will give you ten free hours of my time."

"Why are you so sure?"

"Carol Ann Haley was married to Jim Bud for thirty something years. She wouldn't have agreed if she wasn't absolutely sure there was nothing to find. She knows how things work and she is street smart. She could become the stuff of urban legend herself, if she wanted, except that's not her style. She's one of those old school Southern women, she works behind the scenes and doesn't need applause."

Brass looked down at his lunch and realized he hadn't taken a bite. While Kristin was reporting he thought how she reminded him of Anna Blue or maybe it was the other way around.

"Kristin, what were you like growing up?"

"What does that have to do with anything? Why do you want to know?" Kristin gave him a look that said back off. She didn't like talking about her life and he knew it.

"Were you an only child?"

"No, I have an asshole of a younger brother."

"McCoy said you could have been a lawyer. Why didn't you?"

"What's got into you? Sure, I love the puzzle and interfaced with McCoy's clients. Being the boss doesn't interest me; besides, you don't need law school to be a good lawyer. All you need is a good memory, a willingness to listen with an open mind, an imagination that sees all of the possibilities, attention to detail, the knack of reading faces. Law school can't teach you that. It's innate."

"Why did you strip down for Laurel Moon? Trudi said she would have walked away."

"I thought about it. Something in Moon's eyes said she wanted to see me run. In the end, I was curious about what would happen."

While Kristin was talking to Brass about Laurel Moon, the psychic was thinking about Kristin.

For the second time, Laurel Moon watched the video that showed Kristin from the time she pulled into the lot until she pulled out. The cameras in the entrance hall showed Kristin didn't hesitate when she walked past the donation plate and scooped it up and put it into her bag when she left. Laurel thought that could be a problem. There was only one reason to take the plate: fingerprints.

Years ago, Laurel began tape-recording sessions without her clients' knowledge, video was something new. She'd gotten the idea from a psychic friend who lived in Los Angeles who told her about little spy cameras that could be so well placed that even a cop would not notice them. Laurel called Cousin Dennis and he had them installed for her. Amazing how much more clairvoyant she could be with a little technical assistance.

Moon thought about her clients, the women who could easily afford a hundred a session; sometimes they left a lot more when a piece of information from the ether gave them answers they needed. Often it made the difference in the size of their divorce settlements. Why anyone believed that she had no memory of the session once it was over was a mystery to her.

Longtime clients said she was the only person they trusted. They felt safe and could reveal things about themselves that they would never tell anyone else. Some said it was like they existed in a cone of spiritual protection when in session with her or some other nonsense that Laurel encouraged.

Nearly two years in, McPherson taught Moon a thing or two about the white light of protection and the importance of reading the body language of anyone who came near her. It was the eyes that were the key to reading a person, and those were harder to control than posture or a way of walking and talking. One could fake an outward physical attitude of power or that of a victim, whatever was needed, and maybe fool even an experienced body reader. The eyes, like the saying goes, are the windows.

As Laurel watched the video, she let her mind relax and go back to the first time she saw Kristin step out of her Lexus and walk across the lot. She remembered how her instincts flared. This new client wasn't another rich housewife from one of the high-end gated communities. Women without budgets, she called them. Women who were connected to each other through their husbands' professions, or their clubs, private schools, the salons that gave them all the same look, or the plastic surgeon who gave them the same noses, or filled their lips too large, or their brows so tight they were expressionless.

After nearly thirty years in this business, Laurel was so ingrained into the lives of some clients that they were now bringing their teenage daughters to see her. She had started a new arm of her business. Life coaching was a moneymaker. Her clients who came for psychic counseling also wanted a life coach and that was two hundred a session with a minimum of ten sessions. Whoever came up with the life coach formula for success was right on.

When Kristin stepped out of her car, Moon thought she was looking at a cop or a prison guard. She discarded the thought but it left its mark. Point was, there was something off about this woman. She walked like someone who knew how to take care of herself. When Moon took Kristin's hands in hers and looked into her steady eyes, she felt something was off.

The designer clothing was right on, so was the car, and the handbag. She could stroll into Trey's restaurant and join a cluster of ladies who were regulars there and fit right in. Laurel could see something didn't match up and couldn't figure out what, but she would, given time.

Laurel had planned to stop Kristin at the door when something inside of her said, *Fuck with this intruder, just a little.* Wasn't that why Kristin was here, to fuck with her? She dared to come into her space with dishonesty in her heart. Laurel felt offended by that. She needed to know what the woman was up to and turning her away wouldn't tell her a thing.

Laurel watched the video twice and listened to the recording of the session, trying to get a fix on Kristin. It obviously had something to do with Warren Mitchell and she wondered what this woman thought she could learn from her? Or maybe her presence carried a message or a warning, Laurel wasn't sure, and that possibility sparked her imagination in a way that made her uncomfortable. She picked up her land line and called Cousin Dennis.

Chapter 18

✳   ✳   ✳

MOON COUSINS

D ennis Moon drove out to Laurel's place shortly after he got her call. He didn't pull into the drive where her clients parked. He came in the back way, the way he always did, because it wasn't visible from the highway. He'd bought the two houses on either side of Betty Jo—he had a hard time calling her Laurel—and the property directly behind her.

After her prison experience, she'd had a fierce need to feel protected and he understood that. They were what some might call kissing cousins. As teenagers they had experimented in that way but that was a long time ago and over, completely over. Their fathers were brothers, his being the oldest by fifteen months and Betty Jo was exactly that much younger than Dennis.

Betty Jo greeted him at the door with a hug and a sample of her new blend of pot.

"Dennis, I'm getting a bad feeling about a woman who came to see me." She took a hit and passed the joint to him. She liked to smoke the old-fashioned way, no vaporizers for her, and so did he. "Sit down. I want to show you something." Betty Jo put the laptop in front of him and started the video of Kristin's visit.

When it was over, Dennis said, "You've finally lost your mind. What possessed you?" He was referring to Kristin standing in the pot of water saying a prayer while Betty Jo pranced around her with a fire-breathing bowl.

"It doesn't matter. Here is her license plate number and her cellphone number. I need you to find out all about her."

"I don't need any of that to tell you who you just pissed off. I know Kristin Gilmore. She worked for McCoy for years. She works for a cop now, he's a writer, she is his personal assistant. Bill Brass. He's working the Warren Mitchell case."

"What does that have to do with her coming here? I'm telling you, Dennis, there was something sinister surrounding her aura. That's why I purified her."

"Kristin probably came out here because Brass learned Brenda and her friends were having their Halloween ceremony at Delphi at the same time Warren was in the pond. One of them probably told the cops they got the idea of the ceremony from a psychic and he followed that thread to you. He sent Kristin out here instead of his partner. I can't figure out his motive for that."

"I picked up a strange vibe off her. I confess that my ego ruled my decision to taunt her. I fell prey to my own weaknesses, again." The famous Little Rock psychic took another hit off her joint, shut her eyes, and stayed closed off to Dennis for several minutes. He waited. When she opened her eyes she said, "I am not the one in danger. Isabelle Hart is. She must come see me. Let her know."

"Why don't you call her? She's your client."

"It doesn't work that way. She must seek me. Cousin, I know I was a little out of control with Kristin. Won't happen with Isabelle. She's known to me. I will promise you this, if Kristin messes with me, I will put her purification on YouTube."

"No, you won't! What you will do is destroy that video and all of the others, now. I am removing the cameras. It's got to look like none of this ever happened. Never keep souvenirs. You learned that lesson the hard way back in your younger days and you are too old to learn it again. Now go get every recording of every kind. I'll get started on the cameras."

"I don't get it, Dennis. It isn't a crime to record what happens in my home, is it?"

"Betty Jo. What you don't want to happen is for the cops to find some reason to search your place and confiscate them. There could be things that you wouldn't want cops to know about."

"I don't think that's going to happen. How would she know about my cameras?"

"Not the point. You keep the surveillance running twenty-four seven don't you?" She nodded. "We are being recorded right now. That is my point. You don't know what you've got. It has to go. You don't know how Kristin is going to respond to your humiliation of her."

"What do you mean 'respond'?"

"I'm telling you to shut down your website and blog, today. She will get on there using who knows how many aliases and will cause people to doubt you in more ways than you can defend. She will hurt your business, no, no, ruin it. She called you a fraud. That will be the angle she takes."

Dennis removed all evidence of the surveillance system. He called his tech guy and had Laurel Moon's social media sites shut down. The message appeared that her sites were being upgraded while she was away working with the police in South America helping them solve a kidnapping. When she returned, the sites would be up and running and better than ever. He made a reservation for Laurel Moon to leave that evening for the first leg of a trip that would take her to Costa Rica to visit one of their uncles who had retired down there and then he gave her a ride to the Central Flying service and put her on a private plane.

Chapter 19

* * *

DETECTIVE BRASS AND WARREN MITCHELL

Mitchell was sitting in a reclining chair watching the local news when Brass walked into his den. He pointed the remote at the screen and turned it off. "I was watching my career go down the drain for a second time. People were starting to get over Stanford and now here it is again, interviews with the victims, yack, yack, yack."

"I went by your office," Brass said. "Talked to your assistant. She looked through your desk and couldn't find any of the paperwork you described. The chocolates were not there or the Woodford. The receptionist remembered Jana McKeller. Do you recall anymore about her?"

"I haven't thought about her since we talked."

"I spoke with your pastor. He said Jana McKeller came to see him a couple of months ago when she joined the church, donated five thousand in cash for the playground. She asked about Bible study classes. Pastor John said she attended them regularly. After the last class, which was two days before she met with you, she told him she was going to Oklahoma to visit her brother and would be gone about a month."

Mitchell said, "She did mention a brother in Norman, Oklahoma. When I get to the office, I will look for her paperwork. We filled it out together. She was a really sweet little woman."

"Your lab work came back. You had LSD in your system and a drug that is popularly referred to as the date rape drug which causes memory loss. Are those your regular ways of self-medication?"

"The only thing I take is something for my hypertension and Ambien so I can sleep. Are you telling me Jana drugged me? That's insane."

"We will find out about McKeller. There were several things about the way you were tied that tell us the purpose was not to kill you but scare you."

"Hell, man, I was shot in the arm. Someone was trying to kill me. What do you mean, the way I was tied up?"

"You were wearing an old diver's vest underneath your shirt. The ropes holding you in place were attached to you in such a way you could be quickly released if you fell unconscious and started to drown.

"This operation wasn't carried out by a bunch of hillbillies." Brass didn't know why he used that word, it just came to him. "I know you have seen the news, take a look." Brass handed Mitchell his iPad. He had already pulled up the Hidden Hillcrest site.

Mitchell watched. He saw himself in the pond, wrapped up in tape, like in the YouTube clip, his hands flailing. Then he saw the girl on a surfboard with a paddle. It was hard to see what she was doing, he saw himself disappear under the water, and then she sunk too. He remembered he had tried to use her as a human flotation device because he was so tired. She bit him. He looked at the teeth marks and bruise. Then the man dressed like a soldier appeared in a canoe. That man had mocked him. He'd tied a flashlight around his neck.

"Does that jog your memory at all?" Brass asked.

"I told you the last thing I recalled." At that moment Mitchell could not remember what he had said earlier to Brass. "Wait." He held up his arm. "It just came to me. The girl bit me."

"Why?"

"I don't know."

"You remembered being in the water with an unidentified man who held you around the waist and spoke to you. Your were able to stay awake and keep your head out of the water. You should remember why the girl bit you and remember the man who cut the tape away from your mouth and put the light around your neck. You are holding back information. Why?"

"How can I answer that? I don't remember what I don't remember. I'm suffering from post traumatic amnesia or something like that. I want to know the answers. I want to know who did this to me."

Mitchell had no confidence in cops. If he played it right, he could use them to get what he wanted. "I know you are looking at my clients but you can't know them like I do. Give me time. I know my memory will return. Pastor John said I should find the silver lining in all of this. I think I have. Maybe the publicity will help people know me better, and they will forgive me when they understand what I've gone through myself."

Brass seriously doubted that. He knew if he lost money with this man that he wouldn't give him a second chance. There were too many financial advisors out there who weren't wounded, stupid, or thieves.

"I have never been charged with a crime. I am still in the financial industry. Brenda Katz and Carol Ann Haley still use me and so do most of my other clients. That says something. There is only one person I can think of who has the motivation and the means to carry out this vendetta and that is Isabelle Hart."

"Isabelle Hart? What happened out there took planning, resources, and more than one person. I understand she had motive but you didn't bankrupt her. Why do you think she would want to do this or is even capable? From what you've already said, she has extracted a certain amount of revenge by her lawsuits and complaints. You said it impacted your ability to get new clients."

"Isabelle is a hard woman. Her husband, Dan, was my client and friend for many years. I made him a ton of money. She didn't know anything about investments, spent most of her time in her greenhouse and helping him run his construction business. He was married twice before her and had three girls from his first wife and a boy from the second. There was friction between Isabelle and Dan's adult daughters. He told me Isabelle's memory was long when someone crossed her, and his oldest daughter crossed her several times, and Isabelle got even."

"For example?"

"Dan said Isabelle got Susan fired from her job at Stephens investment firm and she was unable to get work around here after that and it forced her and her family to move to New York. Isabelle ran her out of town."

"Why?"

"I don't remember exactly what the trouble was that made Isabelle so mad."

"How did Dan react?"

"He said he warned Susan not to take Isabelle on, and she didn't listen. I think he said something like, 'Isabelle always plays to win.' Dan loved that about her. She's smart and resourceful. Dan used to call her 'my able lieutenant.' "

"So you don't think Brenda Katz or Carol Ann Haley would do this to you?"

"Hell no! There is not any hostility between us. Isabelle Hart is behind this. Her son probably helped her. His company is doing the road work on Cantrell."

"Do you know her son?"

"No, I do remember Dan said that the kid could operate every piece of equipment his construction company owned. Think about that. Cranes, earth-moving machines, dozers, and all that big stuff. He can operate it. He also flies a helicopter and a fixed wing. He flew his helicopter under the Broadway Bridge and got away with it because he was helping the police search for a body in the river. That takes guts and a strong mind. Ten years ago he was just building his company and today it is worth over thirty million. Growth like that around here is rare unless you've got connections somewhere and operate in the gray areas."

"Do you think he is the man you remember in the pond?"

"I don't know. A guy like that would get someone to do it for him. You said they weren't out to kill me and there were safety measures in place. That sounds like a prank to me, and that is probably how he sold it to whoever he got to do it."

"Did Dan Hart own a gun?"

"He was a duck hunter. We belonged to the same club in Stuttgart. If you are asking about a handgun, he did. I think he had several. He gave me an old

Colt as a birthday gift. It was a collector's item. If you like, I'll have Judy show it to you."

Brass declined. Right now he wanted to keep Mitchell talking.

"He kept a gun in his boat. We'd go cruising the river and he would shoot snakes."

"What kind of gun?"

"I don't know. It was an automatic. That's all I can tell you."

"What about Isabelle?"

"Right after Dan was killed, Isabelle said she didn't feel safe being alone out there on the river and was going to buy a gun and take a course. I told her that wasn't necessary since there were plenty of Dan's guns around and I could teach her how to use them." Mitchell hoped that little lie would give Brass enough so he could get a warrant and go out to Hart's house. Dan told him about the illegal mushrooms she grew and Mitchell prayed they would find her stash and put her in jail.

"Why would she think she needed to buy a gun if Dan had several?"

"I just remember that conversation. I don't know."

"When was the last time you visited the Hart place?"

"When Dan was alive, they would have dinner parties and big outdoor events like on Labor Day. I went to those. I don't think she has had a party since. I heard she completely remodeled the house and has gotten very particular about guests. I liked Isabelle, but Dan and I were friends. I was surprised when she turned on me after the Stanford crisis. If he'd been alive, he wouldn't have abandoned me. She is not the type to forgive."

"So you were inside the house before his death but not after the remodel; is that right?"

"Right. Why do you ask?"

"I am trying to get a better picture of her."

"I know a fair amount about widows. My client base is probably forty percent widows. I don't know of one widow who tore apart the house she shared with her husband six months after he died—except Isabelle. She is a cold woman to do that. My mother didn't move a thing in the house after my father passed. For years, his clothes hung in the closet, shoes placed like he left them, his favorite chair still in front of the television in the den. It was like he was going to come back."

Mitchell was pleased with himself. He could feel Brass wanted to look in the direction of Isabelle and just need a little encouragement. He could sell him on it. That's what he was good at, selling clients on what they already wanted but needed a little push. Like the Stanford deal. Any one of his clients could have done the research on Stanford, and he encouraged them to do it. Some did and were not interested in the deal; others, like Isabelle, Katz, Haley, trusted his judgment because in the past he'd made them lots of money. He often reminded clients that investing is an acceptable form of gambling. Most believed FDIC and SIPC would save them if something went wrong except it didn't exactly work that way. Believing in insurance made clients feel safe so they could sleep at night.

Chapter 20

DENNIS MOON AND BRENDA KATZ

D ennis Moon walked in Brenda Katz's kitchen door with four boxes of Zaza's pizza. Brenda looked like a schoolteacher with four little boys sitting around a table doing homework. "Uncle Dennis," they greeted him, sounding like a choir, and each one came to him for a hug.

"Hey, honey." Brenda bent down a little to give Dennis a hug herself. "Yum." She took the boxes from him, placed the slices on a big platter, and told her grandkids to dig in. She would be on the back porch with Uncle Dennis.

Moon handed her a miniature porcelain box with tiny bird eggs and feathers painted on the domed top, obviously an antique, and probably from one of his pawn shops. She opened it to find it packed with Laurel's aromatic medicinal buds. "Dennis, you bad boy." She stood up and took a small pipe from the top of the door frame.

"This is wonderful, smooth," she said holding the smoke in her lungs. "There is a little taste of anise in there or something. What is it?" She shut her eyes and seemed to forget her train of thought. "Two hits are plenty."

Looking back through the sliding glass door at the boys, she said, "I think I'll go snag a couple of pieces for us. How about a beer to wash it down?"

She touched his head as she passed and went into the kitchen. Dennis turned his cell off. Two hits were perfect for him too.

"Shit," she said, setting down the pizza and beer on the table in front of him. "The princess is here for the boys. Let me get them out the door." She looked at her watch, the vintage Rolex he had given her. "She is forty-five minutes early. The world must be coming to an end."

Brenda scooped up the boys and had them out the front door before her daughter-in-law could get out of her car. It was the princess's habit to sit in her Escalade and text for a while before coming in to get her children. When Brenda's kids were little, she couldn't wait to see them after their long day at school. She brought popcorn or some other snack when she picked them up. Isabelle was the same.

They carpooled together until her oldest got a driver's license. That opened up her day, still sometimes she would pick up the younger ones herself. She loved the energy children brought to her life. The four boys were from her son's second marriage. He was one of those men who started a second family after forty. She saw these old fathers at the soccer fields after school or the T-ball practices. It seemed like they had to prove they were interested.

To her, most of the dads looked like they should have stayed at work judging from their clothes and ears glued to their phones or eyes down at their text messages. They only looked at what was happening on the field when the mothers around them started cheering. So they cheered too and pretended to be present. The young wives of the older men usually came before the practice was over, and they took the children home and the fathers headed back to the office.

Brenda thought that today's children were being turned into the Borg by over-scheduling and constant monitoring by their parents and even the coaches. Dennis called it "the pussyfication of America." There was no such thing as a loser anymore, everyone got a trophy for something.

Dennis was a cute little man, that's what Brenda was thinking when she went back out on the deck. To her he looked like a guy who owned a hardware store in a small Arkansas town, and that was the look he cultivated. Dennis liked to underplay, appear like a nobody, and he was really good at it because nature didn't give him good looks or a great body. She did give him a creative mind.

Brenda sat down and put her hand on top of his. They said nothing, just looked at the view and enjoyed whatever was going on inside their heads and ate the pizza.

"Bren." That was his name for her. "We need to talk about that night at Delphi. Why did Carol Ann shoot Warren?"

"Carol Ann wasn't shooting at Warren. She said she saw a man stalking us and she was shooting to scare him."

"One of my contacts at the station told me there was only Cole, the girl, and Mitchell at the pond, besides you all."

"Couldn't it be possible that she really saw someone and the cameras didn't catch it?"

"There's something we are missing. I think that cop Brass is going to put the blame on Isabelle, maybe all three of you. You girls are all he's got, you were there, the shot that wounded him came from the area of your campsite, you all were clients—still he doesn't have any evidence as far as I know. He may just charge Isabelle if he gets something on her. She's the one who's worked hard to destroy Mitchell's reputation."

"Fuck. Carol Ann and guns. She is obsessed with them. She went out to Isabelle's and they had a little misunderstanding and she drove off shooting her gun in the air."

"Tell me again what happened with the cops."

Brenda went over her visits with the detectives in detail.

"Why didn't you tell Brass that Carol Ann had a gun and fired it because someone was stalking you?"

"I thought we should, but Carol Ann said we better not. She said we'd already lied and should leave it alone. Later, she told Isabelle it was because the gun was used in an unsolved shooting that Jim Bud did. Carol Ann went out to Isabelle's when she was at the police station and threw the gun in the river. Isabelle told me she looked at her security tapes, and Carol Ann loaded a whole bunch of stuff into her boat and was gone quite a while. Isabelle didn't tell Carol Ann she checked her tapes and knew what she had really done.

"The next day the Chinese cop lady came here when I was about to go to work and she wanted my ceremonial robe and accused us of kidnapping Warren. I told her she was full of shit and she could go down to the laundry room and get it and then get out of my house. I'm not dumb. I didn't mind giving it to her. Then the cop said that we were the main suspects but it would look good for me because I let her have the robe, and if Carol Ann let them search her house, it would help exonerate her."

Dennis thought a few minutes. "Carol Ann's story doesn't make sense. If she fired a warning shot like she claims, she should have admitted it. Cops sense secrets. Jim Bud had so many guns, she could have gone home, fired one of them into the ground, and given it to the cops. That would have been better than deny what she did."

"She probably wasn't thinking straight. That man coming after us through the woods shook us up. None of us could hold a thought. I know I couldn't."

"What I think is Carol Ann knew or suspected it was Mitchell and was trying to kill him. She worried the bullet was lodged in his body. That fits. When she found out he was only wounded and the bullet passed through, she couldn't change her story. I want to know how she knew it was Mitchell."

"I don't know how she knew that, if she did. Maybe she accidentally shot him."

"What was she really getting rid of out at Isabelle's? That's what I would like to know. What unsolved crime was she referring to that could be traced back to Jim Bud?"

"Oliver Robertson, someone tried to shoot his dick off behind the stairwell at the river park and Jim Bud did it. That's what Carol Ann told Isabelle."

"It wasn't Jim Bud. You know who he thought pulled that stunt? Carol Ann. He never let on to her he thought it. She hated Robertson because of something he did to a girl who reminded Carol Ann of her dead daughter and worked for him."

"You are not serious. Carol Ann killed Oliver Robertson?"

"I bet Mitchell is going to press Brass hard to blame Isabelle. She's hurt him financially but you and Carol Ann haven't. Mitchell will use Brass as a way to get back at her.

"Brass is a pretty good detective, except he is tired, and he is a writer, and uses cases for inspiration. Look at the one involving that child killer Sabbath Dyme and his con artist wife, I can't remember her name. He got nowhere on that case, but his script sold and is going to be on NetFlix soon.

"In Boulder or Denver or wherever, he didn't solve a case and a child was killed because of it, and he almost quit police work. If it weren't for Marshall Knight, he would not be in law enforcement today. Brass is a wounded man but not a man to take lightly. He thinks like a writer with the background of a cop. He's clutching at straws, desperate to find something. He needs to solve this case. His batting average isn't too good."

"Well, Brass needs to leave us alone, especially Isabelle. Warren got what he deserved. I guess I sound like I am full of vengeance."

"Babe. There are many things about you and me that are different. You are beautiful and I am ordinary. We both hide behind our persona and know how to blend in when we need to. We are like are those little lizards, chameleons. We can only be who we are. You've tried forgiveness. Forgiveness is easier than forgetting, that takes a long time. So I say it is healthy to be glad someone decided to get justice since the law wasn't doing its job."

Chapter 21

BRASS AND KRISTIN

" Laurel Moon shut down her media sites and left town. Strange that she is suddenly called to a foreign country to help their police. My bet is she left because she has something to hide. My visit worried her," Kristin said.

"Worried her about what?" Brass asked.

"I don't know. I could have accused her of assault. She is a felon. The cops go out there. They notice something is off. A warrant is issued. They take a look at her surveillance tapes and find something she doesn't want them to know."

"How do you know she has cameras?"

"The big owl sculpture. Its right eye. The overhead fan with the fancy globe. I noticed those two when she was changing into her purification robe. There are probably more but I didn't have time to really surveil the place. I have a good eye for hidden things. Was great at Easter egg hunting as a kid."

"Why would she take an extreme approach with you, if she had something to hide? That wouldn't be smart. Laurel Moon spent a couple of years in prison;

she'd be cautious. She must have sensed something was off with you." Brass laughed at his next thought, "Maybe that's why she purified you."

"Ha. Ha. Well, she's skipped town and to me that says she is afraid. What did you find at the Hart place?"

"Nothing I could use. As to her mushroom garden, no illegal varieties there. We didn't find any weapons of any sort. Here is what I have to show for my search." Brass held out his hand to show a missing chunk out of the top of his middle finger. "Her bird attacked me."

"You stuck your finger in its cage?"

"What cage! The whole house is one big bird cage. It flies free."

"Yuck! That must be a mess."

"The damn thing is potty trained, Kristin. It only shits in one spot."

"We went out to her place, Trudi showed her the warrant, she opened the door to her house and said, 'Knock yourself out' and sat at her desk with her computer.

"The house is one big room. It looks like that glass chapel Frank Lloyd Wright designed, I can't think of the name. The exterior walls are glass, the ceiling is skylights, no interior walls. You know you are in the kitchen because there is a stove, or in the dining room because of the table, or the den because of the television, no walls. A bookshelf about eight feet high separates her bedroom and bath area from the rest of the house.

"Out of the blue, this bird flies over my head, really close, several times. I could feel the wind from its wings. On its third or fourth pass in my direction,

I held up my hand to guard my head and it lit on my arm and took a hunk out of my finger and flew up to the rafters.

"Hart called the bird by its name, Thor, and it came to her. She put it in what she called the aviary next to the kitchen. His aviary is bigger than my bedroom. It didn't take long to go through the house. The greenhouse and garage were a different matter. That took hours, with all of the equipment and places to store things."

"What about the boat?"

"That is where I felt something was off. The boat was tied up to her dock. I found a bit of dog poop. Looked like someone had tried to clean it up. Hart doesn't own a dog. I asked her when she last used the boat and I felt a hesitation when she at said at sunrise that morning. I think she took the boat out and tossed the weapon in the river."

"Are you having the dog poo analyzed?"

"Yes, and I'll ask Carol Ann for a sample of her dog's. If it matches, Hart will remind me Haley and her dog were out at her house the day Trudi was searching for Haley. Probably a dead end. Analyzing dog shit shows how little I have to go on in this case."

"You think Mitchell was lying about Hart wanting to get a gun?"

"She doesn't have one registered in her name. Dan had several automatics registered, one of them a thirty-two, yet I didn't find a single gun. The casing was a thirty-two. That's how I got the warrant. Mitchell is trying hard to steer me in her direction and I'm tending to go that way."

"What about Katz?"

"Couldn't get one. No residue on her robe. I'm going over to North Little Rock to see if I can stir up anything new. You want to meet Dennis Moon?"

"This case has so many coincidences," Kristin commented. "Moon grew up in North Little Rock and went to school with Manny Walker from grade one through graduation from North Little Rock High. They owned property together. They stayed friends until Manny died.

"As soon as Clinton got elected, Moon and Manny and his brother began buying up property in North Little Rock along Main Street. They figured the presidential library would find its home across the river at the termination of the River Market. The river walking trail crossed over the old railroad bridge to North Little Rock and dovetailed perfectly with the land the three of them bought years before the Clinton library went up. And now their town, once known as Dog Town, became part of the library tourist traffic with a street car and the works."

Brass and Kristin parked on Main and made a pass through Moon's antiques shop. An older gay man let them browse awhile before asking if he could show them something. He introduced himself as Paul and welcomed them and went back behind his desk where he was helping an interior decorator select pieces for a client. Paul knew they were cops, could tell by looking, but he pretended they were a couple, serious customers, and treated them as such. His inventory was top end and that made him proud even though he didn't own one piece of it. They looked around awhile and asked to see the owner. He sent them upstairs.

Brass and Kristin walked into an open reception area where a young attractive woman greeted them. They asked to see Dennis Moon and she didn't ask if they had an appointment or what the visit was about just excused herself.

Moon came out of a side door and introduced himself. He was a short man compared to Kristin and Brass, and a little thick around the middle. He looked, to Brass, more like a clerk than a wealthy business owner. It was his demeanor as well as his clothing. He wore a golf shirt and a pair of pleated pants and loafers. Brass thought he would need to find something distinctive about Dennis Moon in order to remember his face. Kristin, on the other hand, saw his face as sweet with hard eyes. Moon reminded her of an owl. Those birds look harmless with their round faces and forward-facing eyes. In a bird, forward eyes mean predator.

Brass introduced himself as a detective and Kristin as his assistant. Moon knew she didn't work for the department even though Brass made it sound as if she did.

They followed him into his office, a large room with windows looking out on Main Street. His desk was on the wall to the right of the windows where he sat with his back to an antique credenza. Custom bookshelves made of exotic woods lined two of the walls where neat stacks of folders were interspersed with the books. Kristin scanned the titles. Moon had a wide variety of interests. Opposite of the desk wall was a seating area where he motioned for them to sit.

Moon asked how he could help them, and Brass, who had planned to ask the expected questions, didn't. He felt self-conscious and a little ridiculous thinking he could get a read on Dennis Moon. Instead he told Moon what he knew about him and why he was considered a person of interest.

"I've a list of Warren Mitchell's clients who lost money on the Stanford CD's. I've done the background on the women who were at Delphi during the time Mitchell was there. I know that you are dating Brenda Katz and are friends with Carol Ann Haley and Isabelle Hart. Together, the four of you lost nearly ten million dollars from the Stanford scheme. Your friends were at the scene and the four of you have motive. I am guessing you knew Katz, Haley, and Hart were present at Delphi Pond when Mitchell was found in the water."

Moon nodded yes.

"Where were you between eleven the evening of October thirty-first and three in the morning November first?"

"I was in my apartment upstairs." Moon's philosophy when dealing with cops was to act like a witness in court.

"Were you with Katz and her friends at any time that evening?"

"I told you I was home." Moon waited for Brass to go on. If he had anything, he would come out with it pretty quick.

"Is there anyone who can vouch for you?"

Moon picked up a slip of paper and wrote down a name and cell number. "My alibi for the first part of the evening. My assistant Harvey, who lives in the building, will vouch for me the rest of the night."

As background for the question he wanted ask, Brass said, "There are rumors about your connections with the Dixie Mafia. That organization is known for—"

"I know what it is known for." Moon interrupted but didn't raise his voice, kept his tone neutral. "I didn't figure you for the type of detective who conducts an investigation based on rumors, guess I was wrong. I say, you go looking into me all you want, you try to connect me to that organization, fine, just don't come in here thinking you are going to scare me with bullshit. You only arrived in Arkansas a few years ago. You don't know anything about us. Unless you have something intelligent to say, or ask, I believe it is time for you to leave."

"I have a question," Kristin said as she stood. "Did your cousin Laurel Moon play the role of Jana McKeller?"

Moon looked at Kristin and smiled. "I know you used to work for McCoy, Kristin. What I don't know is why you are involved in this investigation. Have you gone to work for the police department?"

Brass said, "I have the same question."

"I don't know Jana McKeller. I can't answer any questions for my cousin. Time for me to get back to running my business." He opened the door to the reception area and waited for them to leave.

Brass needed a moment and was glad Kristin wanted to go into the grocery store at the end of the block. She'd heard that it was even better than the high-end Terry's Finer Foods located near Little Rock Country Club. What she'd heard was right, beautiful produce, high-end products, expensive deli sandwiches, cakes and pies made on-site, and a little cafe inside the store that served excellent espresso and specialty coffee. The tables were full except for one so they sat down and ordered pie and coffee.

"What did I expect?" Brass said. "Only a fool like me would think Dennis Moon would give something away. I thought I would get a take on him; wrong, I got nothing. I can't arrest a guy on the rumors of his reputation. What was behind your question?"

"Laurel Moon dressed up like an operetta version of a psychic when she performed her fire dance on me. She is short and about the right age only heavier than Mitchell described. If Dennis wanted to kidnap Mitchell, what better person to help him than his ex-con cousin?"

"I agree. Got any ideas on how to prove it? About the casing, I'm thinking it was put at the campsite as a distraction, a way to direct us toward an automatic when the weapon was a revolver. Classic misdirection. If only the bullet had lodged in Mitchell's big arm."

Kristin excused herself to the ladies and Brass called the number Moon had given him. He was hanging up just as she returned and sat down.

"It looks like Moon was having a manicure, a facial, and a massage in his apartment Halloween night. I talked to the owner of MediSpa. She will send me a copy of the credit card receipt. Moon takes good care of himself. He gets a massage from Matthew once a week and a manicure and facial every two weeks from JoJo at his apartment. The massage therapist left at eleven-thirty. Moon still has some unaccounted for hours, but we know he has those covered by his man, Harvey."

Chapter 22

REVELATION

Isabelle did not need to follow the search party to the boat, the garage, or her greenhouse to see what they were doing. The tiny cameras placed around her property transmitted images to her laptop. She'd intended to sanitize the boat when she picked up the dog poop but got distracted. Brass had his nose down scraping the floor. Why did he bother? It could be explained, he knew that. He would ask her when she last used the boat? Did Carol Ann use it? And he did ask and got the answers that took him no further in solving the case.

Brass and his search party left the property after making a second round through the garage and greenhouse. Isabelle called Carol Ann.

Isabelle said, "Come out tonight. We need to talk."

At seven, Carol Ann was at her door with a bottle of Don Julio, a fifth of Woodford, and plenty of Vietnamese food. She had Jazzy with her.

"Okay if I stay the night? Plan to get too wasted to drive home. Be like old times when the three of us couldn't stand to be alone."

Isabelle motioned for her to come in and took the liquor to the bar. She measured out two ounces of the tequila for herself while Carol Ann poured the Woodford freely and added a cube of ice. They clinked and Carol Ann said, "What's on your mind?"

Isabelle laid it out for her. "Several things. First of all, after you left the other day, I thought about the things you said. I looked at my tapes and saw you put more than a gun in my boat. You hauled off at least a dozen sacks and boxes. I wonder why you couldn't trust me with the truth."

Carol Ann started to speak, and Isabelle held up her hand. "Let me finish. I went through my old calendars to the day Robertson was shot. Jim Bud was hunting with Danny. Lie number two.

"While we were out at Delphi you disappeared for a long while, said you were looking for a place to pee. After that your energy was restless. I didn't notice you weren't with us when we ran into the woods, until I heard the gunshot. When we got to the car, you were at least five minutes behind us. You told us about the man following us and that's why you fired at him. You asked us, told us, we had to keep it to ourselves if by some strange happenstance the cops found out we were there. I bought the whole thing.

"Now, Brass is looking at me real hard and I haven't done anything wrong except keep quiet about your gun. Something's going on and I think you know what it is."

"Did Brass look at your tapes?"

"Yes."

"What!"

"I had to show him."

"No, you didn't. His warrant was for a gun." Carol Ann seemed to shrink in front of her.

Isabelle waited several heartbeats. "Feel betrayed?"

Carol Ann didn't answer.

Isabelle kept her face neutral—at least she hoped it was. "That's how I've felt since I discovered your lies."

Carol Ann often filled silence with words. Isabelle was comfortable with it and let the stretch of quiet hang between them.

"When I saw all that stuff you put in the boat, I destroyed the evidence. I covered your ass, again, and now I want you to repay me with the truth."

"Are you mad at me?" Tears that started forming when Isabelle said the word "betrayed" now overflowed and ran down Carol Ann's cheeks. Isabelle waited for an answer.

"I shot Oliver Robertson. Jim Bud didn't know anything about it. The day that Brass and Calasa came to our homes, I took everything out of his office. I felt Brass thought we were responsible for Delphi and worried they would search my house. Jim Bud and I had years worth of secrets. I had to destroy all of them. I should have gotten rid of the gun after I shot Oliver."

"What did Robertson do to you?"

"Not to me. It was what he did to women I cared about. He abused them. He was a predator of the worst kind. I confronted him, tried to scare him, and he laughed in my face. I pulled my gun from my purse. He tried to hit it out of my hand. It went off."

"That sounds crazy."

"Just hear me out. You'll understand. Jim Bud and I helped abused women. I wanted Oliver to quit what he was doing to the young women who worked in his office."

"What does that have to do with you shooting at Warren Mitchell? How did you know it was him? I feel like I'm trying to work a puzzle and some of the pieces are missing."

"I didn't. I felt it was him." Carol Ann tossed back her drink and poured another and saw Isabelle was ready to ask more questions. "I'll back up." She took a couple of breaths.

"I was at Brenda's one night. We were waiting on Dennis. You know how she likes to sketch landscapes, people, does little comic books for her grandchildren with superheroes she invents.

"Anyway, we were sitting around waiting for the grill to get hot. Her sketchbook was on the table and I flipped through it. I saw a detailed sketch of Delphi, like an architectural rendering, to scale and all. I turned the page and the next one was like it except it showed a woman with black wings, standing on the dock, holding a fishing pole, a man dangling from the line. His head was just above the water.

"On the next page, another one with three women hidden in among the trees wearing long skirts and shawls, watching the scene. It was a haunting drawing and not like the things she usually does.

"I couldn't take my eyes off it. I actually jumped when she came up behind and touched my shoulder. I made some comment and she said, 'I like to imagine an avenging angel coming for Warren Mitchell.'

"She was smoking a joint. You know how her imagination runs away when she does that. I tried not to think any more about it yet the images kept coming back.

"When I went to find a spot to pee that night, I saw the man in the water. I knew it was Warren. I didn't *know* know it. I *felt* knew it. I saw the sketches in my mind and remembered Brenda's remark. It was the universe speaking to me, showing me, presenting me with an opportunity."

Carol Ann felt her tongue getting loose from the bourbon and told herself to shut up and not let her mouth overload her ass. Then she thought of the nightshirt she'd brought with her. It was black with bold white letters on the front. *I am a Libra woman. I was born with my heart on my sleeve—a fire in my soul—a mouth I can't control. Thank you for understanding.* The words surrounded a drawing in white of a wild-looking woman, her long hair piled high on her head, and an expression on her face that said, *You better believe it.*

The words tumbled off Carol Ann's tongue. "When we ran up the hill, I saw the blinking light. It was my signal. I heard Jim Bud in my head urging me on. I thought I'd forgiven Warren, instead rage rushed all over me. I'd pushed down my great anger and now it was rising up inside.

"I needed Warren after Jim Bud passed, not just about finances, for friendship too; he knew it. You had your son and Brenda had Moon. I was wounded and Warren betrayed me and that is abuse. I could have killed him if I'd wanted that night. I chose to wound him. If he bled to death because of a clotting disorder, well, so what. He was just like Oliver anyway. I don't know who put him in Delphi, but I have a good idea who did, Isabelle."

"Are you pointing a finger at me? I tried to get back at him legally. I wouldn't even know how to orchestrate something like what happened at the pond."

"Maybe you don't. Max does. I'm not asking if you two did it. Those types of questions are best left unasked. If you told me you did, and Brass asked the right question, the lie I would tell might show in my eyes. Secrets are burdens."

Isabelle responded, "You shot a man over a feeling and you think I am the mastermind behind the kidnapping? That is crazy no matter how you explain it." Isabelle got up and paced. She turned toward her old friend, staring into Carol Ann's face. "Who are you, really?"

Isabelle went on a roll, "Brass is after me. He got this whole warrant thing based on Dan having a few registered guns and that casing they found had the same caliber as one of them. Brass accused me of getting rid of the guns. I could get arrested."

"Isabelle, quit being dramatic. Brass is fishing. When we were at the site that afternoon, I was digging a little hole to set one of the pumpkins in and I came across a casing. I flicked it away. That's probably what they found, and they're obsessing over it. Casing means automatic. I can't believe he got a warrant to search your house over that. His imagination is out of control. He is trying to shake you up."

"You said you and Jim Bud helped abused women get justice. So how does that relate to Mitchell?"

"I told you Warren is an abuser, an emotional abuser, and a thief. I wanted to shoot him, not kill him. I felt compelled. That's all."

"That's all! Your 'that's all' has made me a liar to the police. It's brought them to my door. If they trump up something and charge me with kidnapping, are you going to come forward with the truth? Are you!"

"Won't happen. They have nothing." Carol Ann sounded convinced. "We need to stay calm and do nothing."

"How can you be so sure?" Isabelle wanted to know.

"Jim Bud and I knew the law. Keep your mouth shut and you don't have anything to worry about. If you and Max didn't do it, what do you think about

Brenda and Moon?" Carol Ann put that thought into Isabelle's mind as she finished her second drink; Isabelle was still on her first.

"I think Brenda would have told us," Isabelle said. "She can't keep a secret. Hell, I'm just finding out I don't really know you so what makes me think I know Brenda. She went to Laurel Moon first and went spiritual on us, and then we got all into it with her. She wanted to have the ceremony at Delphi. Didn't she? I can't remember. I don't know if Brenda was involved in this. Why would Moon bother? We lost more than he did."

Carol Ann said, "If Jim Bud was still around, he would have already figured this out."

"Life has gone to shit for me," Isabelle said. "Max is dying and Brass is trying to figure a way to blame me for Mitchell. Or maybe it is that partner of his who is pushing it. Brass came by Max's hospital room early one morning. I don't understand why. I can't imagine he gives a shit about me or my family although he acted like it.

"Warren wasn't hurt, and he deserved what happened. Why are the cops even involved? There's got to be more important cases out there. What about that girl who was murdered and dismembered at Alsop Park the other day? That's important. Why torment a dying man and his mother over a nothing loser? I think Brass has something personal against Max."

"What?"

"Max told me how Brass reacted to him when they talked about that stupid buckle I gave Manny for one of our anniversaries. Remember, the one Max hid? Apparently, Brass found it and wears it all the time. Is that weird or what? He took Max hiding the buckle from Manny personally. Something is off about that behavior. I bet he has a dark secret that has scarred his psyche."

"I agree. Jim Bud and I, we knew detectives, street cops, the chiefs here, former cops who went into the PI business, prison guards and superintendents, and Brass doesn't fit. I had a friend look into him a little when he first came around. He doesn't date and he's never been married. The only women he hangs around are his partner and Kristin Gilmore. He isn't gay. So what is he? I mean, what is his private life about? I showed Laurel a picture of him and she did a reading on it. She said, 'He is a seeker and a watcher. A lost man.' Or something like that. Not a cop to worry about in my opinion. He doesn't have it in him."

Chapter 23

MAX WALKER'S FATE

L ess than a week after the cardiac surgeon removed the cancerous tumor living in Max's pulmonary vein, he was released from the surgical wing and
moved to the oncology floor of St. Vincent Infirmary. Before the surgery, the
tumor sent a little bit of itself out to other parts of his body with each heartbeat.
Now that foreign body was gone, except it didn't matter. The tumor had done
its work. Isabelle wondered if it would have been better to have left it where it
resided; it would have broken off and killed him in a hurry.

Isabelle, her daughters, and Carley were with Max when the cardiac surgeon, a neurosurgeon, and an oncologist came into the room to explain to Max
his condition, options, and prognosis. It was felt by the neurosurgeon that there
was a low chance of significant clinical improvement after his series of strokes,
which took out his right arm and leg, one of his eyes, his ability to control his
emotions, or speak clearly, yet left his brain aware of what was happening to
him. The cardiac surgeon congratulated Max for living through the surgery.
The oncologist recommended Max go home, stay comfortable, and prepare to
die.

All Max had to say to them was, "I'm fucked."

Since his surgery, either Carley, Isabelle, one of Max's adult daughters, or his sisters spent the night with him. Tonight was Isabelle's turn and this room didn't have a chair that folded out into a cot like the rooms on the surgical floor. She rolled out her yoga mat and pulled a blanket over herself and slept on the floor.

Around four in the morning, Max slipped from bed and landed on top of Isabelle. His body seemed to move around on its own without orders from his brain. He would migrate toward the foot of the bed where there was not a rail and the nurses would have to resettle him many times during the day and night. Later, as he was further along on the road to death, she would learn the term "terminal agitation." On this morning, she thought he had deliberately gotten up and tried to walk. When she tried to get him to stand, he couldn't.

It took two nurses to get him back in bed. Max reminded Isabelle of Roger, the child of a friend. Roger was born normal. He quit breathing a few hours later and lack of oxygen damaged his brain. Isabelle met him when he was an adult and thought he was retarded; he wasn't. His mother said he had cerebral palsy. He was smart, but he couldn't speak other than to make grunting sounds, his arms and legs flailed, were never still, and his eyes went in two different directions. He couldn't walk, so he was strapped in a motorized wheelchair he operated with the twisted fingers on his right hand. He couldn't use the bathroom by himself and for his entire life had needed a full-time caretaker. She remembered the time Max had met Roger. He'd immediately turned away and wouldn't look at the twisted man. Now, Max was Roger.

The nurse settled Max back in bed and gave him an injection to relax his restlessness. "Max is a hard patient for me. He reminds me of my husband. He was fifty when he died two years ago." The nurse said these words and waited for Isabelle to respond.

Nurses didn't usually say personal things to Isabelle so she asked what happened.

The nurse told the story about her husband who went to the doctor with indigestion and found out he had stomach cancer and the three-year battle to save him. It was impossible, and had been from the beginning, but hope kept driving the family to try. If she and her husband had accepted what was in front of them instead of playing the cancer game, maybe it would have been easier on all of them. As the nurse said, you don't know what to do.

The nurse took out her phone and showed Isabelle the pictures of her husband's decline. In the first picture, he was fit, smiling, a man who owned his own plumbing company. As she scrolled through the photos, he seemed to shrink and shrink until he was a husk. It chilled Isabelle when the nurse said, "This is what is in store. The process will strip your feelings to the bone." She gave Isabelle her cell number and said to call her anytime. "I've been a cancer nurse over twenty years. I know what I know."

It seemed like there was more the nurse wanted to say, but said instead, "I will find a cot." As she turned to the door, she asked Isabelle if she could give her a booklet that would help her understand the dying process. Isabelle felt tears forming as she followed her to the nurses' station and tried to imagine what this job would be like: staying awake when most people slept, watching near skeletons walking the halls like zombies pushing IV poles. The oncology unit was a different animal than the surgery or critical care floors. In those areas there was not acceptance. The drive to keep patients alive was strong no matter what their conditions. On oncology, comfort was the goal and death accepted.

Isabelle accepted the pamphlet *Gone from My Sight: The Dying Experience,* written by a hospice nurse. There was drawing of a schooner sailing toward a distant shore on the front of the blue cover. The nurses called it *The Blue Book.* Isabelle took it back to the room, scanning the pages as she walked down the hall. She read it and when she finished, read it again. She'd already suspected what intuition had told her the morning Max turned up at her house, her boy was dying.

The Blue Book said each person approaches death in their own way, bringing to this last experience their own unique nature.

It was with this blue booklet in her hand as she sat next to Max at five in the morning that Bill Brass had walked into the room.

She'd looked up and said, "What? Have you come to arrest me?"

"I've come to say I am sorry for what is happening to you and your family."

"Why?"

"Because I know what you are going through."

"Are you talking about what you are putting me through or what I am going through sitting here watching my son die or the combination of both?

"Brass, I've learned something while I've been hanging around dying people. Almost everyone who comes here is looking for something from Max. Most of them want to say, or need to, that they are sorry about something from the past and hope to hear a grunt of forgiveness. Believe it or not, most don't know he has cancer all over his body. They think he had a stroke and they expect him to recover. That's what Lollipop, I mean Carley, tells them. So what do you want from Max?" She stressed the "you."

Brass understood her hostility toward him. Hell, he wasn't sure why he was here himself except he wanted to come. What did he want? He didn't know.

Isabelle didn't say any more. She handed him the book and laid her head down on the side of Max's bed and held her son's hand. Brass sat with her, saying nothing, he knew *The Blue Book,* knew that the nurse gave it to her because the time had come for the family to understand what was in front of them. When the clock on the wall turned to six, Brass touched Isabelle on the shoulder and left without saying a word.

As Brass walked down the hall, a small blonde came toward him dressed in running shoes, yoga pants and top, tight, stretchy garments designed to show off her diminutive size. Five foot and ninety-five pounds, he figured. She carried a stack of folders, a laptop, and had a cellphone pressed to her ear. At first he thought he was looking at a teenager. As he got closer, Brass realized he was off by about thirty years. She looked up at him, batted her long, black, false eyelashes and smiled showing over-whitened teeth. Some men might find her cute, like a little Barbie Doll, a toy sized woman. Big head, little body—Lollipop.

The studied neediness in her eyes seemed to say, "I'm just a little woman, you are strong, protect me." Her projection of herself was physical and Brass felt his hand reach out to her. Her arms were loaded, one hand held the cellphone, and it seemed she was reaching out with her free hand and his happened to find it.

The laptop slipped and Brass caught it and the folders before they hit the floor.

She accepted his help and he walked with her in the direction of Max Walker's room.

"Are you Max's wife? I came by but his mother was with him and I didn't want to intrude."

She stopped abruptly and turned around. "I'm Carley. I'll just go into that little private sitting room until she leaves." Her eyes squinted and her mouth hardened when she spoke. It was clear Carley didn't like her mother-in-law. Brass followed into an attractive room with upholstered chairs, a television, small refrigerator, and he sat the papers on a low table and took a seat across from her. Carley asked his name and how he knew Max.

"Bill Brass. I knew Manny fairly well not so much Max. When I heard he was sick, I wanted to stop by." It wasn't exactly a lie. He knew Manny from living in his house with his things. Instinct told him not to explain to Carley how he knew Max.

"You're that detective who worked on the Sabbath Dyme case out at Delphi. Are you doing the latest? I saw the Warren Mitchell thing on YouTube."

"We're looking into it, my partner and I."

"You know Max's mother was a client of Mitchell's and he got her bad, to the tune of three million or so. She is a vengeful bitch. I can tell you that. I bet she had something to do with it."

Brass could hardly believe what he was hearing. "We are interviewing his former clients. She is probably on the list."

Carley batted her eyes slowly to add emphasis, pressed her lips together, made a little sigh, and said, "Put her at the top. I've been married to Max for thirteen years and she's a schemer. Give me your number; I'll find out what Max knows. I would love to see her get her comeuppance. She thinks she is so smart. You need a dictionary to even talk to her—not that I try to anymore."

"How is Max doing?"

"He is just fine. The only reason he's on this floor is he had bladder cancer. MD Anderson cured it. He had a little stroke or two, nothing big. He'll be fine as soon as we get him home. Hospitals make people sick."

Brass couldn't tell if she was lying or so deep in denial that she didn't see the truth. Brass knew Max's condition was terminal. He only question was, how long would he live? A month, three, six would be a stretch.

Max Walker's wife accusing his mother of kidnapping Warren Mitchell played into Brass's thinking on the case. He'd considered the Moon and Katz aspect but it didn't feel right to him. Moon had the means but Katz didn't have the hate. Isabelle Hart did, and she hatched the plan and her son carried it out. Part of it anyway. His gut told him someone else took care of the kidnapping. Walker probably anchored Mitchell in the pond and subcontracted out the kidnapping.

"The Warren Mitchell incident happened on Halloween night. Where were you and Max?"

"Surely you don't think I would help Isabelle do anything. If she were drowning, I would not throw her a lifeline."

"You were the one who put her name forth as a suspect. She had to have help. Where was Max?"

"Uh. Let me think. I was taking the kids to trick or treat, earlier in the night of course. I think he was checking on a job for a while. He has a job going that works at night and he looks in on it. So I know he did that. He goes to bed early. Gets up at four. So he was either checking his job or asleep on the couch."

Couch? Brass wondered what that said about their marriage. "I see. Is he really close to his mother?"

"Close? I don't know how to answer that," she said in a tight, high voice. Carley turned away from Brass, stood, paced, and spoke without making eye contact. "She better be out of his room by now. She doesn't know when to leave." Turning around to face him, Carley continued. "Yesterday afternoon, she was sitting in a chair next to Max when I came in. I asked her for some privacy. I like to get in the bed and snuggle with him when I visit. She said, 'I'll give you Japanese privacy,' and didn't leave. What the hell is 'Japanese privacy'? Typical of her. I didn't know what she was talking about. So I left and told her I would be back in an hour and she said she would be gone by then. She's a bitch.

I can say that to you. I see in your eyes you are a kind person who doesn't judge. I appreciate that, and thanks so much for helping me carry my files."

Carley walked toward the door, leaving the folders and her laptop on the table.

Brass picked them up and followed her down the hall to Max's room and set them on the stand next to his bed. "Call me if I can be of help." He handed her his card and said goodbye.

Late that afternoon, Brass stopped by the Whitewater for a beer and to get a sense of the place. It captured his imagination right away. He couldn't have written the scene better. The conversational noise lowered as regulars stopped talking to check out the stranger who had stepped inside the dimly lit bar and grill. The history of the town hung in black and white framed photographs on the wood paneled walls, signed photos of presidents from Carter to Clinton, state senators, representatives, Central High, and so on.

Cigar and cigarette smoke hung in the air but it did not cover of the aroma of ancient and deeply imbedded grease in the paneling. In a booth along the back wall, he recognized a state senator having a drink with a young, well dressed woman. A contractor type sat at the bar flirting with the bartender. Brass guessed she'd been in that profession since 1980 and was still good at it. Brass ordered a Bud Light, a beer he thought of as piss, because it was on tap. He was sure they didn't have a Belgian ale in the cooler.

As Brass sat at the bar, the place started swelling with men and women who looked like they worked as lawyers or government employees from the state capitol and its surrounding offices just up the street. He was about to leave, when a man walked in and the bartender called out to him, "Hey, Moon. The regular?"

He answered, "Two. Got company on the way."

Dennis Moon took the last available booth. He couldn't see Brass from where he was sitting. Within minutes, Brenda Katz walked in looking like a high-end lawyer on a mission. She scooted in the booth next to Moon and planted a kiss on his cheek. Those two just didn't fit as a couple in Brass's mind. Moon was practically a gnome. Katz was a good-looking woman for her age, or, as his mother would have said, a handsome woman.

There was something baroque about this case, the dramatic style of the crime, characters with ties to Manny, Delphi Pond, Anna Blue, all of it. He thought of a series he'd read once about two old detectives, in their eighties, who still worked for the London police in what was called the Peculiar Crimes Unit. They solved crimes the old-school way, intuition, historical knowledge of the city and its inhabitants, no tricky high-end forensics.

As he thought about the old detectives, he realized this case would have to be solved the same way, on intuition, uncovering the history and secrets of those connected to Warren Mitchell. Brass couldn't go in a linear direction to find the answers. He needed to create a map with contour lines and roads that led to unexpected places to solve the mystery.

There was so much going on, so many secrets, underneath the kidnapping and torture of Mitchell. In Brass's mind, Mitchell had it coming, and he wasn't really hurt except for the wound to his arm. Brass kept reminding himself to act like a cop. He really should quit the force. Then there was his partner who needed coaching on how to get along with the inhabitants of the South. When he went on one of his internal rationalizations of why he was doing this or that, his bullshit meter often hit red. Like right now. Trudi and her needs were way down on his list of reasons not to quit. He was a detective because he liked playing the game, and he could use what he learned to write the scripts that supported his lifestyle.

His grandmother would have been proud of what he had accomplished with his writing. Growing up, his mother left him and his sister with his dad's mom once a week while she had her "day off." They watched two soap operas with Mamaw in the afternoon. She called them her "stories" and said this was her "time out." She made him and his sister sit in front of the television and gave them a bowl of popcorn. When he started school, Mamaw would ask him to write stories and read them to her. He was still doing that, except now the stories were called scripts and his grandmother was long gone.

Mamaw had been an old woman at forty while Katz was in her mid sixties and still had lots of life left. She wore high heeled shoes and tight suits. Mamaw wore an apron over a faded, shapeless house dress. She worked as a maid at the church across the street from where she lived with Roy and their seven kids. Katz was an accountant and worked with her husband. They were partners in a successful firm.

Brass's grandfather, Roy, was an engineer on the railroad, and he was also an entrepreneur. In the1950s he'd built what would by 2016 be called "small spaces." Roy moved parts of old buildings to his backyard and turned them into little houses. He rented them to couples. The extra money allowed Mamaw to quit working at the church. By that time, her knees were worn out and she was old before her time. Brass didn't know that until later.

Brass was thinking about Mamaw when Brenda Katz passed next to him on her way out the door. Moon stayed in the booth.

The waitress brought Moon another drink and an order of fried shrimp in a basket. Brass wouldn't be sitting in this bar now, if Max Walker hadn't mentioned Moon, Dixie Mafia, Whitewater. The talk stimulated his imagination. What was the motive for mentioning this place? Ironic, Max in a hospital bed while Brass drank beer in this bar.

Chapter 24

* * *

MONGOOSE

"What do you make of this?" Brass asked Trudi, handing her a sheet of paper.

She studied the photocopy of the letterhead, a mongoose running across the top of an internet address on letter sized paper. Below the logo, a photo of Warren Mitchell kneeling in front of a stained glass window with his shirt off flagellating his back with a riding crop.

"Where did that come from?"

"Don't know. The desk sergeant brought it to me this morning," Brass answered.

"This looks like St. Edward Church. That's Station of the Cross number ten."

"How do you know that?"

"Brass, I was raised a Catholic and you never recover from it. I went to a funeral there with Greer. That's a place to start."

"You take the priest, or deacon, or pastor, or whatever those guys are called."

Dennis Moon would have agreed with that if he'd heard the plan. He wanted Brass to pay a visit to the victim. Moon had given the cops hidden tips over the years, and the game was to give just enough. Too much and a smart cop could find his way back to the source. It was noon, and he was taking twenty minutes out of his day to put his feet up on his desk, lean back, and let his mind wander over past events.

Dennis remembered the first time he'd met Isabelle. It was a week after her high school graduation. It was Manny's first date with her, a blind date, and they had met up with him and his new wife, Sandy, for miniature golf. Three months later, Manny and Isabelle married.

They hung out together as couples for the next ten years: going to clubs, dinners, the drag races, fishing out at Manny's grandpa's place in Cabot. Then Manny and Isabelle split, and she married Dan Hart. Soon after, Dennis and his wife divorced. Manny and Dennis remained friends until he died. It was not until Dan died, and Dennis began dating Brenda, that he became re-acquainted with Isabelle. He often saw Isabelle and Max at the Whitewater; eventually, he and Brenda joined them for drinks and then dinners. It reminded him of the old times with Manny.

Moon thought about Brenda's drawing of the angel dangling the man in the water. It was then he knew she had not forgiven Warren for the betrayal; she had hidden it from herself in the form of forgiveness. Brenda said the idea of the sketch came from a dream and now that dream was eating at her. He was half kidding when he told her to visit his cousin Laurel Moon for an interpretation. She went, over and over again.

With the help of Laurel, Brenda remembered "The Dangling Man" sketch didn't come from a dream but a vision she had out on the grass watching the river run past and tripping with Isabelle on her magic mushrooms.

The trip opened up a new spark of creativity and for days she couldn't put down her sketch pad, sometimes staying up half the night and filling page after page with angels, men, water, until the one she called "The Dangling Man" appeared. She named the series of sketches, *River Dreams.*

Dennis looked at his watch and on cue, Brenda walked in talking, "Isabelle and Carol Ann appeared at my door at five this morning. I am so afraid they are going to arrest Isabelle."

She sounded like tears might be next so he put an arm around her, walked her to an overstuffed chair, and poured her a stiff drink.

"The police spent a couple of hours over at Isabelle's lookin' for Dan's guns, and Brass accused her of destroyin' evidence when she told him she was out in her boat that mornin', and he wanted to know about Carol Ann and the boat, and he was suspicious because there was nothin' on her security videos and . . ."

"You're running on and not making any sense. I'll ask questions that will help organize your thoughts. Okay?"

"All right."

"How do you think Carol Ann found out Warren Mitchell was in the pond?"

"I wondered that myself. Isabelle asked her why she shot Mitchell. Carol Ann told her about the sketch I did way back when. Said when she saw the man in the pond and he seemed to hang there, suspended in the water, that the sketch flashed into her mind. She had a vision it was Warren. When we ran to the woods, she saw the blinkin' light and took it as a signal that she needed to take a shot at the man in the pond. She felt it was Warren; she didn't know it was."

"What happened this morning that's got you so upset?"

"Carol Ann asked me outright if I hired someone to kidnap and water torture Mitchell. Said the whole thing looked like my creepy sketch. I told her that was the craziest thing I'd ever heard. I told her it looked to me like it was her idea. She was the one who shot him. Then she pushed me backward, and we got into a cat fight and Isabelle had to pull us apart."

"Then what?"

"She said I didn't have proof she had a gun. If I went to the police, they would have her word against mine, and they wouldn't believe me because of who I dated." Brenda started to cry. "It was awful. We are keepin' her secret about the shooting and she is blaming me for Warren."

"What did Isabelle say?"

"Nothin'. After a few minutes or so, she started laughin'. The real kind that makes you snort. Said she wished we could have seen ourselves on the ground like animals. That broke the tension."

"Then?"

"I thought Isabelle was going crazy when she started laughing—Max on his deathbed and Brass stalking her, who wouldn't have a breakdown. She also just found out Carley has a lawyer and is planning to stop her from having Max's health care proxy, and . . ."

Dennis interrupted by making a little shushing sound like you would to a crying baby. "Stop. Settle down. Stay on point. We can talk about Max later. What happened after the tension broke?"

"Isabelle told Carol Ann not to worry about us. We wouldn't tell on her because it would get us in trouble."

"That's right. There's nothing to worry about. I promise. Just let it play out and don't panic," Dennis assured her.

Brenda didn't ask why he thought that because she knew ignorance is sometimes a good thing. Dennis would not have told her anyway, if he knew.

"Thanks, babe. I feel better now. This whole thing is so, what is it, a bad trip. How did we get into the middle of this drama?" She checked her watch. "Got to get out of here, grandmother duty."

Moon's landline rang. He picked it up and listened. "Calasa just left the church."

Trudi texted Brass as she walked out of St. Edward's. Brass was waiting for her when she came in the station eating a sandwich.

"What did you learn?"

"I talked to Father O'Donnell. He wouldn't say much until I showed him the photo. That opened him up. He's been worried Mitchell was having a breakdown although he had not witnessed him beating himself.

"He first met Mitchell when he came to him and asked how he could become a Catholic. This happened shortly after the Stanford mess hit the papers. O'Donnell does the early morning Mass and Mitchell has attended it every day since they met. He has found Mitchell kneeling in front of the Stations of the Cross after Mass, especially the crucifixion scene, almost every day. He said Mitchell showed interest in stories about saints that suffered. That sort of thing."

Brass recapped. "He goes to the big fundamentalist church and teaches Bible class. He attends Catholic service every morning, studies for conversion. He beats himself in front of a religious icon. Sounds sick."

Brass continued, "I showed Mitchell the photograph; he said it wasn't him. I asked to see his back; he refused. I pointed out the scar on his cheek, and he said his head was probably photoshopped in the picture.

"I let it go and asked him about the mongoose letterhead. Claimed he didn't know anything about it. His wife pulled in as I was leaving, and we talked before she went into the house. She confirmed it was Mitchell flagellating himself, that he was 'searching for forgiveness.' I said, 'Isn't he a victim too?' She said he was guilty of ignorance and the hardship it brought to his clients and his family. Right on script.

"I wanted to say if Warren feels so bad why doesn't he sell this big house and give the money to those clients who are suffering. They live in River Ridge, gated with full-time security guard, custom houses. Bet his house is eight thousand square feet. It is paid for. He took care of the mortgage, over a million, a week before the news about Stanford hit the papers."

"That is suspicious. What did Kristin come up with on Mongoose, besides it being a small carnivore that was introduced to Hawaii in the early 1800s and didn't kill rats like it was supposed to?"

"She didn't mention that bit of local knowledge. Basically, it's a company for thrill seekers. Those who can afford to pay a big fee for someone to scare them senseless in a controlled way. Get yourself kidnapped, or shot at, or robbed, that sort of thing."

"I've heard about those. Did she speak with anyone about Mitchell?" Trudi asked.

"No. Doesn't work that way. The site gave some information on how to contact them, and she had to fill out a form and wait for someone to get back to her. Kristin had what they called a pre-interview interview. To continue, she would need an appointment with a consultant in their offices in Madison, Mississippi, or to pay one to come to her.

"I called down to Jackson, talked to a detective acquaintance. He seemed to know quite a bit about Mongoose. They make arrangements, for all kinds of human needs, besides the need to feel fear, and they have a top-notch detective and security team. Kristin and I are flying down in the morning."

Dennis Moon knew more about Mongoose than Brass would ever know. It was an arm of one of the Moon family businesses down in Mississippi. He held in his hand a copy of the contract Mitchell signed with Mongoose. He didn't actually sign it but that was beside the point. An expert in those matters did, and it would pass inspection, if needed.

The next morning, after a private flight to Jackson, a Mongoose driver met Brass and Kristin at the airport and took them to the upscale office park where the Mongoose offices were located. The receptionist led them back to a private interview room and introduced them to their consultant.

Brass showed his credentials and asked to see the manager.

Danielle Dawson looked to be a former athlete, maybe a college tennis player, or basketball. She came across as confident and sure of herself. She answered his request with, "Absolutely no problem. I will call and verify your identity; if you are who you claim to be, I will make the introduction if she is available."

Kristin asked, "Who will we be speaking with?"

"I will inform you once we've completed the process. I would say thirty minutes. You are welcome to wait here, or we have a Starbucks in the office center. I can text you."

"We'll stay here," Brass said. "Miss Dawson. Are you originally from Mississippi?"

"I am. Why do you ask?"

"I don't hear a hint of a Southern accent."

She smiled. "I speak with clients from all over the world. Being without a regional identifier in my speech was a prerequisite for the job. Now I will see to your request."

"She sounds like a robot to me," Kristin said after Danielle left the room. "Regional identifier, I guess that is the politically correct term for accent."

Brass cut his eyes to what looked like a small metal sculpture hanging on the wall to the left of Kristin with a collection of other art items. She got the message, camera.

"Let's go by Starbucks. I'm still on Arkansas time." She laughed as she said it, letting him know she'd gotten the message.

Brass had stood up to leave when the door opened and Danielle Dawson walked in and asked if they would like a beverage while they waited. Brass told her to text them when his background check was completed. They were going to the coffee shop.

"Brass, I think she wanted us to stay so they could monitor our conversation," Kristin said as they walked across to Starbucks.

"Then she shouldn't have given us an alternative."

Twenty minutes later, he got the text and they returned and were led into the office of Katherine Wolf. She dressed in expensive dark blue slacks, tailored to fit, jacket that molded perfectly to her medium chunky frame. She wore a high collared white blouse, a triple strand of pink pearls, and stud earrings to match. Her hair was pulled back into a low clipped ponytail. She appeared to be in her mid fifties although it was hard to tell. The sags that were expected in the neck and along the chin line of a woman that age were apparent otherwise her skin was clear and flawless, almost unwrinkled around her blue green-eyes and full mouth.

There was something in her eyes that reminded Kristin of Laurel Moon. Maybe it was the color or the way this woman looked at them. What had she read about the Dixie Mafia? Didn't they start in Mississippi?

"Glad to meet you, Detective Brass. Believe it or not I know all about you. You are famous." Her cadence was definitely Southern but she didn't drop her "g's" like Katz often did or pronounce her "r's" hard. Wolf ignored Kristin.

"I expect you would since you wouldn't see me unless you verified my identity."

"In our business, we are careful who we help. I meant the Sabbath Dyme case. Read all about it. And your scripts too. You are talented. To get it on the table, I also know about the Warren Mitchell business and your investigation. I am guessing that's why you're here."

"Why is that?"

"Don't play coy. I know about the Mongoose tip. You are here because of it. You want to know if Warren hired us to give him a thrill. We have detection and security divisions here at Mongoose that rival those of many countries. Most of our men and women worked in the government. We pay better. The thrill business is a tiny part of what we do. It was a small thing for me to find out about what you and Kristin Gilmore, your personal assistant who has nothing to do with the LRPD, are looking for. By the way, Kristin, McCoy is an old friend of mine. How is he doing in retirement?" It was not a question she expected Kristin to answer, and she didn't.

Brass felt a little dizzy. "Did Warren Mitchell sign a contract with Mongoose?" He couldn't think of anything else to ask.

"I'm not going to tease around." Katherine Wolf handed him a copy of the contract.

Brass looked it over. "That was too easy."

"Suit yourself. Do you want to solve this one or have another unsolved case on your record? Not too good for a cop's reputation, the unsolved. Up to you. I think we are all finished here." With that, she stood up, opened her office door, and Danielle promptly escorted them out. Wolf called her contact as the door clicked shut. "It's done."

Not until they got back into the rental car did Kristin speak. "Someone wants you to have the reasons to let this case go. Question is, do you want to? In my opinion, Mitchell doesn't deserve the time it would take to find out what really happened. Maybe his soul needed this. Well, maybe not. I think I am still feeling the effects of my purification session with Laurel Moon." She laughed.

When the small jet landed back in Little Rock, Brass and Kristin went to the Flight Deck restaurant and bar for a drink. Brass checked his cell, multiple text and voice messages from Trudi; he wasn't in the mood to report to her.

"Brass, fill her in on what went on. Maybe the pings will stop," Kristin said as she excused herself for the restroom.

Trudi answered his call with a hard edge in her voice. "I've only left you seven fuckin' messages, sucka."

He hated that pidgin or whatever her local talk was called. He used to think she was saying "fucka" when she called him that name. He didn't like working with a partner, but the chief wanted him to train her in Little Rock ways, and he couldn't turn Marshall Knight down on anything. They were friends and he owed him.

"I didn't listen to them. What's up?"

"You're kidding. Mississippi? Mongoose?"

Trudi was angry with him because he took Kristin and not her on the Mongoose interview. Although his reasons were sound, Trudi couldn't accept them. Besides he'd saved the department the price of the tickets. He paid for their rides in a private jet. Knight was okay with that. He'd known Kristin for years and he valued what she brought to any investigation. Knight's department got her for nothing. Brass had his own way of sussing out a witness or a suspect, and it didn't match up with Trudi's way of handling things.

"What's the deal? I'm your partner and you take your *special assistant* on our investigation. Bad enough, even worse since you didn't bother to call and tell me what happened."

"Am I sensing a little jealousy?" he teased.

"You thought she could pick up on some vibe down there that I couldn't because she is a Southerner, and I'm not, right?"

"Look, Trudi. You like to go in hot with heavy background on a witness. Sometimes, I like to go in without my intuition and impressions being influenced by Google. I didn't want you getting sideways with the Mongoose people like you did Isabelle Hart. I didn't trust you could keep your cool." Brass was tired of playing nice with her.

Trudi kept silent.

"We just landed. Meet me at the Red Door in thirty minutes and I'll fill you in."

The line went dead. He didn't know if she would show. Kristin returned to the bar and he said, "Got to tend to my partner. Let's go."

Chapter 25

TRUDI'S THEORY

Brass was hungry for his favorite comfort food, a cheeseburger with onion rings and a Stella from the Red Door. He wasn't a Big Orange or a Brave New Restaurant fan—they were too gentrified for him. Trudi was waiting for him in the parking lot when he pulled in. They walked in together without speaking. The building was at least fifty years old and showed it, along with its upgrades. It had a wacky charm, having gone through many incarnations: a boutique furniture store, four different restaurants, a dress shop, a gallery, and so on.

When the Red Door came with its home cooking and old-fashioned bar, it had been an instant hit in the neighborhood and had stayed that way for over fifteen years. It was owned by the chef who owned Casanova, the Italian restaurant next door that shared a parking lot with the Door. The owner called them sister restaurants and used this combination of local home-cooking and Italian at two other locations in town.

Trudi knew what Brass would order. He always ate the same thing at the Door. She occasionally went there with him, and when she did, she usually ate chicken and dumplings and strawberry shortcake when it was in season. It was

Ron Cole's favorite eating place too, especially after he'd spent a couple of hours at the shooting range. She'd been thinking a lot about Ron Cole lately.

They seated themselves and Brass opened his backpack, took out a folder, and handed Trudi the original Mongoose contract signed by Warren Mitchell.

The waitress sat down his beer with, "Here you go, honey." Brass winked at her.

"It was all too easy. Something's off." Brass poured the beer into its special glass chalice.

"You don't believe this contract is real?"

"No, I don't. Someone wants us to leave this case alone and is giving us an easy out. I think it means we are getting close."

"Are we? I don't think so. We have four, maybe five, imaginary suspects and not a shred of evidence against any of them. Speculation is all we got. Maybe someone is trying to do you a favor?"

"Imaginary? Favor?"

"We're looking at the wrong people, Brass. Why haven't you looked at your buddy Ron Cole? You thought he was the mystery man who beat up Sabbath Dyme and locked him in Connie Horton's shed, but you didn't pursue that thread." She waited for a comment and got nothing. The waitress set down his burger and onion rings without a word. She knew an intense conversation when she saw one.

Trudi continued, "You're making the same mistake here as you did with that one. Don't you find it strange that Delphi Pond is the site of two recent crimes and Cole is involved with both in some way? The Blue kid wakes up in the middle of the night and paddles her board out to the center of the pond. Cole happens to show up. What was he doing out there?

"He said he saw a light on the pond and was curious. I don't buy that. Two people on the pond at the same time, at night, and they run across a man who is wrapped up in duct tape. I think Cole was the one who put him there, didn't plan to kill him, just scare the shit out of him, and was keeping an eye on him, and then the Blue kid comes into the picture. She was a complication.

"Who does Cole call? You. Why not 911? Do you know if Cole was aware that the widows were planning a Halloween party that night? I bet he did. He patrols that place night and day. If he did, then he schemed up his plan for Mitchell to occur on the same night. He used the widows as cover, a deflection, in case he needed one. He has it all under control until that kid shows up.

"What does he do after putting that flickering light on Mitchell? He heads to the bank where he knows the widows are, scares them into the woods, and follows them. They become our chief suspects, and we never asked them if they knew Cole. We're looking at these sixty-year-old women and no one is looking at Ron Cole."

Trudi waited for a reaction. Brass chewed his food and kept his eyes on hers.

"Cole gets some buddies to come up with those pictures of Mitchell in the church, and then they magically turn up at the station. How convenient is that? We—no, you and Kristin go to Mississippi and are handed the contract with Mitchell's signature. Is it going to take another crime at Delphi Pond for you to figure him out? Brass, Cole is a sociopath. He did this."

Brass spoke in his flat tone. The one that had intimidated Trudi when she first started working with him. "When did you come up with this theory of yours?"

"It's been in the back of my mind all along. I've been busy following your lead and not thinking on my own. For a while, I thought you were onto something with the widows and Hart and her son in particular. It is too complicated though, too many characters, too much like a made for television movie. It is too much like one of your scripts, to be blunt. The simplest answer is usually the correct one in police work, most of the time anyway."

Brass finished his burger and rings before picking up the thread. "What do you have to back up your theory? What ties Cole to this, aside from him being on the pond that night, which is not unusual for him? What's his motive?"

"He doesn't need one. He's crazy. I have nothing on him regarding Mitchell, but I have a hell of a lot of history on him, his military background, his connections in the private security business. This would have been a piece of cake for him. I can't prove it. He's too good of a planner to leave anything behind. The only thing he couldn't control was the Blue kid. We have nothing on the widows, or Moon, or Walker either."

"Would you consider that Mitchell hired Mongoose to scare him and this has nothing to do with Ron Cole?"

"No. I don't buy it. That Mongoose contract is something Cole has come up with. It's his gift to you. If you accept it, you've solved the case and he gets away with it. If we get proof that is Mitchell's signature on the contract, then I am wrong. When we confront him, and if he did have a contract, Mitchell will say he didn't know what the thrill was going to be. He never imagined it would be kidnapping and water torture. If he had known, he would have told you. Or maybe he says he didn't hire Mongoose and sticks with that story. If he wants to clear what is left of his name, he will need to prove that's not his contract."

Brass said, "We have at least three possibilities. The widows had motive and did it. Ron Cole did it because he is a sociopath. Mitchell did it to himself through Mongoose. Hell Trudi, maybe Cole works for Mongoose."

"I am saying Cole did it. There are not any other possibilities that make sense.

I've had it for today, anyway. I'm going to the gym and then to the movies with Greer. It's not life or death, is it? Someone has given you a gift. Are you going to take it?"

"What do you think, Trudi? What should we do?"

She stood up to leave. "Aloha a hui hou."

"That doesn't sound like an answer to me." Brass supposed she'd said, "I'll see you later," but wasn't sure. The only word in the sentence he knew was "aloha" and that meant hello and goodbye in a crazy language that didn't even have a full alphabet. No wonder she wasn't normal. As he was thinking about Trudi, and her Ron Cole theory, she walked back into the dining room and stood over him.

"Why did you visit Max Walker in the hospital? You'd already visited him at his office. What's that all about?"

"You sound like a jealous wife. It doesn't suit you, Trudi. What I do with my time outside of the job is none of your business."

"It is my business. Walker is a suspect."

"I think I just heard you say the only suspects in this case are in my imagination, and I don't have a shred of evidence against anyone. I suggest you go on to the gym and the movie. After you do that, we will sit down and go over what we do and don't have in this case and make a decision where to go from there."

Trudi started to speak. He spoke before she had a chance. "I'll walk you to your car and call it a day."

Chapter 26

*   *   *

MAX'S WORLD

M ax laid in the hospital bed knowing everything that was said and going
on around him, but he couldn't react. He could speak one or two words
at a time so he kept his communications simple. He didn't have a choice. Max
saw a movie once, well not all of it, it was too disturbing to finish, about a man
who had a massive stroke and nothing in his body worked except his mind. He
was an observer to his own life no longer a participant. Now he was that man
and with that thought tears streamed down his face.

Carley was snuggled up next to him like she always did when anyone, nurse,
doctor, or visitor, came into the room. When the tears came, his visitor left,
leaving him alone with his wife. He wished he could kick her off the bed but
his legs wouldn't obey. Once his knee hit her in the chin and made a bruise: he
only wished he had been in control of the blow. It had been Carley's foolish idea
to move him to a different hospital when his mother had first brought him in;
Carley had convinced him he should go and he could never forgive her for it.
Now Max knew the time lost moving to the university hospital and back again
was what had led him to this state. He would have been a dead man either way,
but at least he could have spoken for himself in the time he had left. Now his
wife was going after full health care proxy and he couldn't even stop her.

"What's wrong, Maxie? Just let me lick those tears off your handsome face." She leaned over him and he could smell her breath. "Are you crying because I know all your secrets now? I got into your trust documents, and I don't like one bit what you planned for me. Well, I have plans for you too. I'm in charge now and you are getting your well-earned comeuppance. How does it feel, sweetie?"

He wanted to say, "Go brush your teeth and use some mouthwash." It was too much trouble.

His mother walked in. That was Carley's cue to leave.

He grunted, "Hi," pause, "Moma."

He thought about his mother, his sisters, his kids, Carley, Richard Blue, his friends, his companies, his employees, his predicament. He had nothing else to do all day except think. His mind worked even better than before. The downside was he couldn't take advantage of it.

The first few days after his operation, the effort to get a few words out had been exhausting, and his mom had told him, "If you don't want to talk, keep your eyes shut, people will think you are asleep, and you won't have to try." That was good advice and he kept them shut most of the time when unwanted visitors came. There seemed to be a train full of people who wanted to see him. He felt like a zoo animal, a tiger or panther, in a cage.

Max thought about his big miscalculation and the cause of it—guilt. He knew it to be true. "Guilt is a choice, a useless emotion," his mother always said. She drummed that into him and his two sisters. "It will cause you to make bad decisions." This was one of the guidelines she taught them to live by. He'd learned another of her rules when he was about five. He'd hit his mother because she made him wash off the crayon figures he'd drawn on his bedroom wall. In response, she knocked him to the floor. She grabbed him by the shoulders and got into his face. "Two lessons you better learn early: When someone hits you, hit back twice as hard. And don't start a fight you don't have a chance to win."

In his mind, he ran down the list of Moma's rules to live by, most were on how to stay a few steps ahead of everyone. The one about guilt was hanging around because his final bad judgment was based on it.

He was thinking: *If only I'd gone for the body scan. I finally got my primary care doc to order it in spite of what the high-end MD Anderson cancer doctor said, and then I cancelled my appointment to go to Cici's dance contest, or pageant, or whatever those events are called. The little girls look like they are practicing to become pole dancers and strippers. Ten-year-olds in skimpy tight costumes hunching around to music with lyrics about sex. The auditorium was probably full of pedophiles in the balcony.* He'd felt guilty because he usually didn't go, and he had cancer, and on and on, so he didn't take the test that would have saved him from this fate. Moma was right, guilt made for bad decisions.

The evidence was right there on his brain scan. Little clots all over the top of his brain that started forming months ago. That's why he'd felt off, some were breaking away. If only, if only, if only he could have taken his helicopter out and crashed it into one of his quarries he wouldn't be living in hell. He was paying for that mistake. He wondered if this was the universe's revenge on him for all the revenge he'd dealt out to others who had deserved it. For those he hit back harder than he'd been hit. He couldn't decide if justice and revenge were the same thing. The legal system uses the justice system to make offenders pay for their crimes against society. When individuals do the same thing it is called revenge. All sorts of thoughts swarmed around Max's mind all day and night, and he couldn't seem to shut them off any more than he could use his legs.

"Moma." Isabelle squeezed his hand to let him know she heard. "Please. Kill. Me."

Isabelle leaned in close when he said her name. "I am working on it."

"I. Don't. Want. You. . ."

Isabelle interrupted, "I know. You don't want me to go to jail for you. Don't keep talking. I will go tell the nurse you are in great pain before Carley gets back here. That way you can get some rest."

Isabelle had put her ear up close to Max when he started speaking and then whispered in his ear. Carley had hidden cameras in his room. The iPad on the table next to the head of his bed that played his music was set up so she could be out in the waiting room looking at her computer, seeing and hearing what was happening in the room. Isabelle thought about telling the nurses but decided to wait until she needed to play that card. Let Lollipop have her little games.

Isabelle was aware of her daughter-in-law's need to feel important, and now she felt that way. Carley flew in a private jet to Houston, smart doctors spent valuable time talking to her, all of the medical lingo she was Googling, everyone telling her what a good job she was doing helping Max get well. Carley craved attention from Max and now she was getting it from his sickness.

As the pain medication started to take effect, Max began to imagine himself waking up dead, walking into the Pearly Gates, where he would find Manny and his first dog. The least The Great Spirit in Everything could do was give him a massive stroke to strike out all of his brain function so he wouldn't have to think. If he couldn't think or feel he might as well be dead. Once that happened, Moma would have all the machines shut off and see to it he died as quick as he could. Carley would fight her on it, take it to court to keep him on machines forever. Carley would lose. Moma played to win.

Max's mind wandered in the direction of Warren Mitchell and the investigation. He was worried Brass would blame his mother. He didn't like that cop and resented that he had the nerve to show up at the hospital that morning he fell out of bed. He'd kept quiet so Brass wouldn't know he was awake. He wanted Brass to talk, but he didn't say much of anything. Something was off with that cop. He knew Moma would figure it out.

As Max was thinking about Brass, Dennis Moon pulled into the parking lot. He hoped there wouldn't be a line of visitors for Max. He'd come at various times over the past several days, trying to get a few minutes alone with his old friend's son. Dennis had known Max since he was a baby. The friendship he had with Manny was still going strong when he'd died. It felt right to both of them, he and Max, keeping up with each other, keeping Manny alive by talking about him.

Moon opened the door to find Isabelle Hart preparing to leave the room.

Isabelle hugged him. "Moonie." They held each other like friends do when each needs a hug.

"I wanted to come by and see Max. I used to say to him how much we, me and him, had in common. If he hadn't of been so handsome, I would think he was a Moon."

"Our connections run deep, Moonie. It would take a map to understand them."

"I need to tell Max a few things."

"I understand. I'm out the door anyway." She whispered in his ear, "There are cameras hidden in the room. Carley's doing."

Dennis was not expecting a two-way conversation. He knew Max's limitations. His mind was working and his body wouldn't obey. Moon was thinking as he stood next to Max's bed that it hadn't been that long since Manny died and now he was saying goodbye to his old friend's son.

Dennis sat on the side of the bed and put his hand on Max's arm. He kissed the top of Max's head and whispered whatever words friends use when they say this kind of goodbye.

Max's head moved from side to side and Dennis saw that his face was working to say words. "Hi. Moon. Glad. You. Came."

Dennis got close to his ear. "Max, I know how sick you are. I know you are worried about your mom. I want you to know that plan B is in place. There's nothing for you to worry about. She is safe. I will keep an eye out for her when you're gone."

Max whispered, "I. Love ya. Moon. Thanks." Moon saw the tears drip down Max's cheeks and felt his own rising in his eyes.

Dennis walked out of the room, looked right and saw Brass and Carley walking toward the room. They saw him too, but he kept going in the opposite direction. What did that mean? Those two together? He would ask Betty Jo what she thought. Carley Walker frequently consulted the psychic and had for years. That reminded him to call and let his cousin know she could come back home. Laurel, Dennis couldn't figure out why she called herself that. If she wanted to pick a flower it should have been a hydrangea, that was more her body type.

Chapter 27

* * *

BRASS AND COLE — HART AND BLUE

B rass usually entered the Red Door from the back patio but this afternoon he went in through the door painted red at the front.

"Hey, Brass." The bartender nodded her head to indicate where Cole sat with both elbows on the table, eating a sandwich. A tall glass of iced tea sat in front of him along with an empty shot glass. He sat where he usually did with his back to the corner. He saw everyone who walked in through the front and from the patio.

The bar was empty of customers except for the two of them. Three in the afternoon wasn't a popular time.

The bartender came over and set down a beer for Brass and handed him an envelope.

The greeting card–sized envelope looked like an invitation with the gold embossed name of an art gallery on the flap. He laid it on the table thinking he would get to it later.

Cole got to the heart of the visit. "I guess you wanted to meet me because your partner's been hanging around Delphi. She was there the other night talking to the BigRock crew, coming to my house, talking to the neighbors. She's trying to make me the bad guy."

"I know about her theory. I haven't tried to change her mind. She's stubborn."

"Calasa wanted me to explain why I left Mitchell in the water alone. She said that my actions were abnormal. I told her I left Anna to guard him. He was conscious, strong, and I was not his keeper. I needed to scout out the three figures I saw.

"She said I created a 'clever diversion' chasing after the women. Said I was trying to shift her focus to them. I asked her what she thought my motive would be and she said the pleasure of torturing someone. That it went right along with my sociopathic personality disorder."

"Trudi. Have to admit she is an original. I guess that's the way they grow them out there in Hawaii."

Cole put a mock serious look on his face. "This will be her next theory. I can hear her pitching it to Marshall Knight.

"Chief, Detective Bill Brass is the mastermind who designed the plan to kidnap and torture financial advisor Warren Mitchell. He set the stage out on Delphi Pond because he knows Ron Cole and his habit of checking the perimeter of the pond and the houses that surround it at least twice a day. Brass figured if something unexpected happened, and Cole was on the pond at night in his canoe, like he usually was, Cole would call him instead of the cops. Cole doesn't like to get involved with police. He likes to handle things himself because in his demented mind he is still in special forces. Brass maneuvered the investigation of this case like he did the Sabbath Dyme case. He sets up crimes to solve them and then write scripts. His motive is money and fame."

Brass said, "I think that is my favorite. I like it better than the theory the widows dreamed it up, or Max and his mother did it, even better than Mitchell hired a thrill company to torture him. I really liked Calasa's theory that Ron Cole did it because he is a sociopath, until now. Cole, this theory is the winner. Thanks, buddy."

Cole wiggled two fingers in the air and the bartender brought over two shots of bourbon.   They clinked the glasses and tossed it back. Brass picked up the envelope and took out the card. Looked at it for a while before he spoke.

"It's a picture of a painting on the front of an invitation to a party at the Starving Artists Cafe at six tonight."

He handed it to Cole. The photograph was of an oil painting. Three women in long robes standing between tall pine trees on the bank of a small body of water. There was a full moon in the sky; its glow illuminated a figure in a canoe who was looking at an angel with wings spread wide, standing on an outstretched tree limb, dangling a man at the end of a line into the water.

"What the fuck is that about?" Ron handed it back to Brass.

"Guess I'll go on over to the Starving Artists and find out. Doesn't give me much time to get ready."

"It feels like a taunt. Like, can't you see what is in front of your face?"

Brass used his phone to take a picture and send it to Kristin, asking her to find out what she could about it. From the style, from what little he knew of art, it looked like something old, or trying to look old. The lighting reminded him of Gottlieb's *George Washington Crossing the Delaware*. He remembered it from years back in art appreciation class.

While Ron Cole and Bill Brass were discussing theories, Isabelle Hart was visiting with Maria Blue.

Maria called to check on Max, and Isabelle asked her to come by for lunch. They lived less than ten minutes from each other. She knew Isabelle from the Twenty-Eight Hundred Club, had friends in common, but they didn't socialize, too much age difference and not enough of the same interests, and that made the invitation unusual. Maria got the feeling Isabelle had something on her mind besides her dying son.

Maria pulled up and Isabelle met her at the gate. She welcomed Maria into what she referred to as "my tree house," led her up the stairs, and offered a variety of drinks ranging from a Chopin vodka martini to homemade lemonade. Maria followed Isabelle into the kitchen where Isabelle put the glasses of lemonade on a tray and handed it to Maria while she carried the lunch tray, hummus, olives, toasted pita chips, Greek salad, and went outside to the deck. The weather was good for early November, warm enough to sit outside in the middle of the day, too cool to sit out at night.

Isabelle started off the conversation. "I first met your husband when he was a freshly minted accountant. Manny and Max were two of his first clients at Mark Griffin's accounting firm. Did you know it was Max who encouraged Richard to go to law school?"

"I think I remember he said one of his clients suggested it. We were just getting started on our careers and it seemed to me accounting was a good profession. Why add to it?"

"Max convinced Manny to give Richard the money to go, and your husband worked it off in legal work. Good for both of them, don't you think."

Maria didn't want to admit she didn't know about that. All these years she thought his mother had paid for law school. She wondered what that said about her marriage.

"I don't remember if he told me or not. That was a long time ago. It is a tragedy about what has happened to Max. He is only three years older than

Richard." Maria felt uneasiness stirring in her because of what Isabelle said about Richard and wanted to get off the subject. It didn't work.

"Max has a trust that Richard drew up for him. The document was looked over by another attorney, Dick McCoy, trusts are his specialty, you probably know him. He told Max that in his fifty years of lawyering, he had never seen a trust like it. McCoy questioned Max about why he wanted to over-manage the lives of his widow and children yet give his trustee unlimited discretionary power to make decisions. Max told McCoy all he was interested in knowing from him was whether it could be broken or not."

"I don't understand why you're bringing this up. It's not my business, or yours for that matter."

"Wait here." Isabelle left the table and came back holding the document. "I want you to read the marked pages."

Maria set the pages facedown on the table. "Why?" Maria didn't need to read them, but she didn't want to let Isabelle know she already knew about the trust thanks to her daughter.

"Strange, you're not curious. I asked you to read a document that will affect your future but you don't seem to care. Makes me wonder. You already know, don't you?"

"I feel like I am butting into Richard's business, breaking the confidentiality code. I'm a jury consultant and it's not ethical."

"Bullshit." Isabelle waited. Maria looked down at the pages. She picked them up and read.

Isabelle said, "If I were the wife of an attorney who had agreed to take on this much responsibility for a man's widow and small children for such a long period of time, I would have wanted him to tell me. It might be attorney-client business, still it is your life too. This arrangement will affect you personally. I know how much money Richard is going to make from being trustee, and can guess how much income it is going to bring to his law and accounting practices, so I understand why he took on the job. This is his retirement plan."

"So you're saying you are doing me a favor?"

"I don't know. Maybe I am the kind of woman who wants to help another woman who is going to need it. Fuck. I don't know why I do anything these days. I'm operating on instinct. I feel compelled. I remember when you used to show up at the Twenty-Eight Hundred Club. Was that fifteen years ago? I liked the way you told a story. One night, you described what you were going through trying to have another child, the fertility treatments, the mood swings. You told it Chris Rock style, funny and pointed. I was also there the night you decided to quit treatments. We cheered. You had guts.

"Your husband is too involved in Max's life to be an objective trustee for his estate and that combined with his great discretionary powers could cause problems like McCoy warned. Max made me trust protector and that means if there is a disagreement between the beneficiaries and the trustee, I am the one who decides. I want things to go smooth, and Carley is going to put pressure on Richard to get what she wants. It won't take long before dealing with her is going to wear him down. If you know what is going on with Richard, it will make things go smoother for him, you, me, my adult grandchildren. It is like Max created a big web that has us all connected together and we didn't know about it much less agree to participate."

Maria said, "I think I would like that martini after all."

Isabelle went inside to get the makings for it and when she came back out to the deck Maria Blue seemed lost in her thoughts.

"Isabelle, you've had so much going on with your son and this investigation over Warren Mitchell. I heard you and Max are their main suspects, is that right?"

"They are saying I thought it up and Max carried it out. Brass has a writer's imagination. To save what is left of my sanity, I have decided to think of this as a game, a soap opera, a diversion. He has nothing on me because there is nothing. I think Brass is jealous of Max. That's what behind this."

Maria looked puzzled.

"Let me explain. Brass bought my ex-husband Manny's place. He has kept everything of Manny's like he found it. He even discovered a silver, handmade, belt buckle hidden in the fireplace. Max said, when he told Brass that he had hidden it from his dad over thirty years ago, the look on Brass's face was pure anger. He thought Brass was going to punch him in the face. He felt Brass took it personally, almost like he was Manny's son not him.

"It was right after that happened, Brass started doubling down on us. Max said he thought Brass had lost sight of the case because he wanted to punish him for hiding the buckle. I know it sounds nuts, but I think Max is right. Brass has twisted himself into knots trying to prove it was us. Almost like a jealous brother."

"Isabelle, I know Brass pretty well. My daughter, Anna, is a Nancy Drew type, and she talks to Brass quite a lot. He is very patient with her, acts almost like a mentor. It started with the Sabbath Dyme case. Anna was spying on Dyme and his wife and took pictures of her fall from the deck. That helped clear him. Brass and Anna have talked every day about the Mitchell case. As you probably know, Anna was the one who found him.

"I believe even if Brass could prove you were the instigator, and given what has happened to Max, he wouldn't charge you with it. I heard him tell Anna, 'Kidnapping is serious and so is shooting a man, but Mitchell is not going to die from it.' Brass gets it.

"Like you pointed out, the tentacles from Max's fate have entangled all of us. You are losing a son, his children are losing their father, his sisters a brother, my husband, as you said, has agreed in many ways to take on a second family. Anna described Warren Mitchell as the financial husband to his widowed clients. Well, I say, Richard's role as trustee for Walker's estate is that of financial husband on steroids.

"He will pay all of the household bills, credit cards, maids, repairs, and so on. Things Carley should know how to do. Is Carley incapable of managing her life? Or is she being punished? Is it revenge? Is it a little of both?" Maria wasn't expecting Isabelle to answer, and she didn't. She was on a rant and Isabelle didn't interrupt her. "Carley gets a monthly allowance and something extra at the end of the year, if she obeys. That's how you treat a child. I get what you are saying about how it will affect me and our marriage. There are many opportunities for drama. Sister wives pretty much describes us."

Maria saw the big picture, Isabelle thought. She realized people often protect themselves by agreeing or saying they understand, when in fact, they feel the opposite. Isabelle wanted it to go smoothly for all involved. Time would tell. She'd done all she could.

Chapter 28

✳ ✳ ✳

BILL BRASS AND
ISABELLE HART

After days of going back and forth, spending long hours day and night in Max's room, Isabelle referred to the hospital as "planet-of-the-sick." Populated with patients, visitors, medical staff, ancillary people who work in the coffee shop, gift shop, cafeteria, the place had a rhythm that didn't match what was going on beyond its walls.

Once Max was released and went home, the rhythm of his house changed. His sick-room was set up with full-time nursing staff, a hospital bed, medical supplies, Carley's spy cameras. Friends and visitors came in and out all day. Isabelle thought the only good thing about his coming home was his young children could see him anytime, snuggle in the bed with him, watch television with him, and pretend everything was going to be okay. Max was home less than two weeks before he was re-admitted to the hospital, and Isabelle found herself falling back into her former visiting patterns and the habit of eating meals at nearby restaurants.

The visitors tired Isabelle. It seemed they came for themselves. She often warned them, "Maybe you might not want to go in," but they did, and most came out shocked by what they saw. Max's personal trainer was a perfect example. She explained what he would see, and the man said that Carley had told him that Max was just fine. In less than one minute, the trainer was back out of the room, looking pale, saying to her, "I wish I hadn't gone in there. I didn't realize." The young man didn't know Max had terminal cancer. He thought Max had a small stroke because that was what Carley had told him, told everyone. Isabelle told him the truth. It was after this encounter that Isabelle needed a little respite. Leaving Max with his sisters, she left his room and went to the Big Orange for a drink, or two, and something to eat. The restaurant was less than two blocks away and the food suited her.

It couldn't be but it was. Brass walked toward the door of Big Orange as she was about to open it. She wondered if he were following her and decided he was. They sat down at the bar; he ordered a Duvel and she a double Don Julio, neat, and a Stella.

"Looks to me you are needing an escape."

"What a fine detective you are proving to be by noticing my drink order, deducing what is on my mind, a regular Sherlock Holmes."

He smiled. She said nothing.

"What's happening with your son?"

"He is on a respirator, not doing so well."

"What does that mean?"

"He had another stroke, a massive one. Took out half of his brain stem and all cognitive functioning."

"This whole thing's gone down so fast," Brass said.

"Yeah. When Max went home he was cognitively intact. He couldn't carry on a flowing conversation, but he let the physicians know he did not want chemotherapy and his goal was to stay home and be comfortable.

"I supported his decision, but Carley and Richard Blue, Max's attorney, didn't. Blue told me he thought if Max had a five percent chance of recovery, then he should fight. So what if he wouldn't ever walk, and had to wear a diaper, or couldn't speak clearly, and his body was wracked with seizures, and his eyes, when opened, wandered off in two directions, and when someone walked into the room he cried. He personally could live with that and he thought Max should too. I told Richard, Max isn't interested in existing like that, and it wasn't his job to have an opinion on what Max should do or not."

"My worst fear in life is what's happening to your son," Brass said and Isabelle could see he meant it. Who would want that? Maybe those who thought it was *The Lord's will*, but she wasn't one of those and neither was Max. The Lord wasn't part of their lives.

"It's not a coincidence you are here. What do you want, Brass?"

Brass didn't know what he was doing there. He'd felt compelled. So he didn't give an answer, just said, "I don't know about losing a child. I don't have any. I do know how the cancer journey goes. I've been there with my mom, and it, well, I don't need to tell you what it takes out of a family."

"Especially if the wife, or husband, doesn't honor the dying person's wishes. Did you have to go through that?" Isabelle asked in a flat tone. She couldn't sense how real he was being.

"I did with my father. He was in total denial. I was twenty-one when it happened, Mom was forty. I had her health care power of attorney. He fought me. We haven't spoken since she died. He said I killed her."

"With Carley, I am not sure if it is denial or if she wants to keep Max alive because as long as he is breathing, she has the checkbook. Once he passes, Richard Blue is in total control of her financial life."

"I can't imagine Carley told you that," Brass said.

"Her actions tell me what's on her mind. When Max was home, Carley removed his pain patches, hid his medications, and told the nurses to give him Tylenol for his pain. She told visitors he was overmedicated. One afternoon I came over, his body was in spasms, his blood pressure was stroke level, he was crying and begging for pain relief, and she wouldn't unlock the safe. I told her I was going to call adult protective services if she didn't give the nurse his medication and she refused. I dialed it up on my cell, showed her the number, and she gave in."

"That's not good for the family dynamics, I would imagine."

"When the surgeon and other physicians gave Max his diagnosis and prognosis, Carley and Richard started on a mission to get him back into MD Anderson and finally did. Max agreed to go. Said he wanted closure. Kamat, the doctor who treated him for bladder cancer, had been refusing to see Max but finally arranged for another oncologist at the center to review his case and see him. Richard hired a medical jet to take Max to Houston. It cost twenty-five thousand dollars for a one-way trip. Imagine. He and Carley took a private jet down. Richard and Carley were expecting Max to stay and they were wrong.

"The chief of oncology saw Max. She did not examine him, or order further tests; she had all of his records, slides, images, reports, and that was all she needed. She told Max they would not treat him; he was terminally ill, there was no treatment that they could give him to save his life. There was an experimental treatment that could build his immune system but due to the damage already in his brain, it could, as she put it, 'fry' his brain and he would not recover. His cognitive function would be destroyed. She recommended palliative care and sent him on his way."

Isabelle took a long pause and then tossed back her double tequila and slugged down her beer and held up her hand to show she wanted another round.

"The medical jet brought Max back to Little Rock the next day. I wasn't notified until two days later. Max developed a fever during the flight, his breathing was labored, his blood pressure high, and he was taken straight to the emergency room. I found out he was back and in hospital through a friend who worked there. I asked Richard why he hadn't called me. He said, 'Carley wants you to leave her, and the children, and Max alone.' You can imagine how that pissed me off. Evidence he was taking sides.

"I went to the hospital as soon as I learned Max was there. The oncologist thought Max would benefit from the treatment the physician down at Houston did not recommend. He gave Max the first treatment the day after he was re-admitted. Max agreed to take it. I don't know if he wanted to do it because he hoped it would fry his brain or what. I didn't get a chance to see him before his mind was gone. I blame Richard Blue for that. I doubt I will ever forgive him. As predicted, Max stroked out, then had a heart attack, and now he is on a respirator in critical care. Extraordinary means are in place now, and I am the decider of his health care. I told the doctors to shut it all down. Let him die as he wished."

"What do you think is going to happen?" Brass asked as he indicated with his forefinger he wanted another beer.

"Carley got a TRO when I did that. The judge will order extraordinary measures be kept in place until we go to court for an emergency hearing, and that will take about a week. The judge will decide if Max's wishes are carried out. I predict Max's attorney, Richard Blue, won't show up. My lawyer, who by the way was the criminal defense attorney who got Sabbath Dyme out on the Alford plea, will present the facts using the testimony of the doctors which will show Max is terminal and not cognitive. Max will win the right to die. Then I will put him in hospice, palliative care only, and I predict he will die within a week. No one knows."

"Why do you think Richard Blue won't back you up? You're acting for Max."

"Richard worked his ass off to get Max down to MD Anderson. He and Carley are on the Miracle Team. Richard won't be there. He would have to choose a side so he will make an excuse not to come. Max is going to die and Richard Blue doesn't want to get on the bad side of Carley."

"Why would his wife want him to survive with those limitations?"

"Please. As long as Max is alive, Carley has the checkbook. I told you that. When he dies, Richard Blue takes over as her financial husband. She has no power. Maria Blue will have a sister wife and she already knows it. I told her."

"So does Carley know about her loss of financial control when Max dies?"

"Max always kept his business secret from Carley. When he had the first strokes, she took his computer from him; he couldn't focus on the screen any-way. She has access to his documents, something she has never had in all their years of marriage. She knows what is in his trust. Think about it.

"Free spending and showing off are important to Carley. She is one of those wives without a budget. Why else would she persist in keeping Max alive when she knows he hates what is happening to himself? Aside from the free spending, she is getting even with him for what's in his trust and for the thirteen years he basically ignored her."

"You see her as a cruel person. I met her. She seemed caring to me."

Isabelle glared at him. "Brass, even a moron can understand what is going on with Max's health given the information the physicians have provided. Carley acts like a child. Denial is more acceptable than the truth. What would her friends think if she told them, 'I don't want him to die because Richard Blue will be in charge of my life forever when he does.' "

Brass had no words. Her words had taken his away. He didn't know Isabelle Hart could speak at such lengths. She usually spoke sparingly around him. They sat in silence for a time.

"I need to get going," he said. "Will you be okay driving back to the hospital? I am sure you are over the limit. I'll call you a cab." She looked and sounded fine to him but he thought he should make the offer.

Isabelle turned him down, told him she was none of his business, but he could arrest her as soon as she pulled out of the lot if he wanted to go down that road. Then she said, "You still didn't tell me why you tracked me down. Never mind. I really don't care. It was good for me to rant a little. I deserved an audience, and you are a good listener. Cops usually are. So you know, Detective Brass, I realize there is something off about you. Please, leave me alone. If you aren't going to arrest me, stay out of my life. I don't need your sort. I really cannot tolerate you."

Brass was stunned and hurt by her words. He paid his tab and left a larger tip than he intended. As he walked out the door, he was overcome with a sadness he didn't understand.

Chapter 29

STARVING ARTISTS CAFE

The Starving Artists Cafe was located on North Little Rock's Main Street. It was a popular lunch spot for the people who worked in the offices across the river in downtown Little Rock. The cafe was run by the former chef and the office manager of Trey's restaurant, owned by Connie Horton whose grandfather created Delphi Pond out of a swamp.

Brass arrived a little after six with his invitation in hand. The cafe was crowded with people enjoying the complimentary cocktails and appetizers. The talk was lively. He looked around to see if he knew anyone and was surprised to see Anna Blue and her mother in conversation with Chief Marshall Knight. Anna saw him before he could reach the bar where they were standing and came toward him.

"Isn't this exciting? There are thirteen different pictures on the invitations. They are the thirteen dream interpretations that the artists produced. It was a contest sponsored by the art department at the university. They are affiliated with the cafe."

Anna was her normal self, running like a racehorse, streaming information. "Let me see yours." Brass handed it to her. "It is the same as mine. This means something. You are here because of the case. I knew it the minute you walked in the door."

A waiter appeared with a beer and a mug on a tray. "Mom ordered that for you. All the drinks are free. I have a fresh squeezed limeade."

"Fill me in." Brass smiled, ready to hear Anna's thoughts. He was happy to see her, especially after the encounter with Isabelle Hart. He added to Hart's worries. What could he expect?

"I will put it in context. About six months ago, the Starving Artists program announced their new project. Wasn't that right around the time Max Walker first discovered he had cancer in his bladder? Anyway, people from Pulaski County were asked to submit a dream, a committee would choose thirteen, and students would interpret the dreams in their paintings, or whatever. Six students in the art program and one teacher would bring the dreams to life. The dreamers are here anonymously. The work is for sale, and all of the proceeds except for one dollar goes to the scholarship fund at the art department. The dollar goes to the landlord here."

"Who is that?"

"Just wait. Back a long time ago, Dennis Moon, Manny Walker, and Manny's brother bought up most of Main Street, including this building. After Manny died, his brother approached the art department with the idea of a collaboration between the university and the owners of this building. The owners would donate the space for one dollar a year to the university to use as an art gallery and sublet part of the space for a restaurant. The deal was the restaurant was required to show works of art the university selected on its walls. The artists also had to agree to be present every day at lunch to do their painting, sculpting, photography, whatever, in a space near the entrance of the restaurant. The proceeds of the art sales would be split between the artist and the school."

"When did you get your invitation?" Brass asked Anna.

"Mom got her invitation two weeks ago and so did everyone else. Dad was supposed to come with her except he had a client emergency. Max Walker is dying in the hospital and his wife needed my dad. So I came instead. Now you are here and we have the same picture on our invitations. That is not a coincidence. Marshall Knight has the invitation with a naked woman wearing red high heels standing in a doorway that is floating on a stormy sea. I love that one. The person who put Mitchell in the pond is here. I feel it. What we need to know is whose dream is on our invitation. It depicts the crime scene. I have many thoughts about this event. We need to talk more about it later."

"Why are there only thirteen works?"

"Six students, two works each, and the professor does one? Here comes Mom. She saw Isabelle Hart today. You should hear about that. Mom is, well, upended by it all."

The chef at Starving Artists and his partner walked up to the little stage where the artists did their lunchtime work. The lights dimmed for several seconds, making the place go nearly silent.

He explained what the evening was about and how the school would benefit from the auction proceeds and then he invited everyone into the formal gallery.

Anna, Maria, and Brass walked in behind the other guests to a large white space, high ceilings, gallery lighting, the floor carpeted in black wool. Six paintings hung on each side wall and one on the back. Each was covered with a black velvet cloth. The students stood next to their works.

The art professor introduced himself and his students, not all were college age, some were in their forties and already worked as artists but were taking his classes. He explained the artist would read the dreamer's dream.

The first dream was read. "I dreamed I was flying above a desert. Something had been stalking me and that's how I escaped it. I took flight. I came back to earth inside a crater. It felt peaceful. I was now a young girl with flowers in my hair. The night was starry with a full moon coming up. I felt safe until I sensed something behind me, a menacing shadow. In the dream I commanded myself to wake up and I did."

The artist, a young man, unveiled the thirty-six by forty inch watercolor of a young girl standing on a rust-colored cinder cone in a volcanic crater, looking beyond at an even larger gray cone and the mountains beyond the lavender and pink colored floor of the crater. The night sky was black and filled with stars as a full moon was starting to rise beyond the far side of the crater. Her waist-length hair was laced with yellow flowers and her skirt was made of stars. Brass felt moved by the stark peacefulness of the dream until he noticed the black panther stalking the girl from behind. Its eyes were glowing, set on her, and its body was made of feathers. He wondered why he hadn't seen the menacing creature right off; instead, it was the last image his eyes found. That told him something about himself, but he didn't know what.

Eleven more readings described eleven works of art: acrylic painted on smooth board, oils on canvas, photographic montages printed on aluminum, scenes painted on silks and hung on frames used to hang Japanese obis, a ton of imagination and talent on display. Brass was waiting for the piece he'd come to see—the one hanging alone on the back wall. He thought it would be the one on his invitation. The whole Starving Artists show was a stage play created for him; he knew it, and so did Anna Blue. Cole was right. This was a taunt or a finale.

The professor stood next to the last work. "The dreamer has asked the dream not be read. The dreamer wants each of you to interpret the piece for yourselves, to let it speak to you without prejudice from the reading of the dream."

He removed the covering with the flourish of a magician, revealing the biggest painting in the show, five by seven feet of oil on canvas. The audience took in a collective breath. It was the most disturbing dream in the collection.

The painting glowed. The full moon in the sky—there wasn't one that Halloween evening—shone through the rising fog hanging over a small body of dark water. The tall pines reached toward the night sky as three figures stood next to them. There was a figure in a small boat on the pond and the light from the moon illuminated it. The figures were looking at the same thing. Standing on the tip of a big oak limb was an angel with yellow wings spread wide. The angel held a line in its right hand and from it dangled a man. The terrified man's head hovered just above the water. His eyes were turned in the direction of the viewer. His face was a mask of fear, eyes stretched wide, showing the whites of them, his open mouth shaped like the terror he was feeling, like a soldier dying in battle.

Anna said, "If this was painted before Warren Mitchell was kidnapped, the dreamer actually made his or her dream of revenge come true, if it was a dream at all. I think the doer of the deed set up this auction. Maybe the others were dreams, but not that one." Anna squeezed his arm. "I bet that professor was told what to paint and paid good money under the table to do it." Brass was thinking the same thing.

"We thought about a silent auction," the professor said, "but decided this amazing exhibition of collective thought and talent deserved to be heard. So I am pleased to introduce Little Rock's own auctioneer Buddy Coyne."

Buddy stepped forward in his jeans and boots, string tie and plaid shirt, and started the action. The first painting went for five thousand and the next eleven hovered around that amount. When it came to the star of the show, bidding started at ten thousand. A representative from Crystal Bridges, the Walmart gallery in Bentonville, held up his hand, and then bids went in five hundred dollar increments until a bidder stopped the action with twenty-five thousand, and Buddy declared it sold.

"Who was that woman who bought it?" Anna looked at her mother, at Brass, all around the room, hoping to see someone her mother knew speak to the bidder. The woman was short and a little overweight and seemed to disappear in the crowd around her. They milled around for a while until they were the last to leave.

"I am going to talk to the professor who painted *Halloween Prank*. Love that name. Find out when he painted it and what he knew about the dreamer. I'll be right back, Moma."

Maria turned to Brass. "Maybe you could get her a summer job working at the department. What are you going to do about this case, Brass?"

"What case? I don't have one. I know when I've been beaten by a superior player. Here comes Anna. I can see on her face, she didn't locate the professor. Let me walk you ladies to your car."

Dennis Moon stood looking down at the street below as the Starving Artists party broke up and the guests made their way to the parking lot. Brass, Anna Blue, and her mother walked together.

Chapter 30

HALLOWEEN PRANK

Dennis Moon's private residence was on the third floor of the building across from the Starving Artists Cafe. The view was spectacular, the river and the lights from downtown Little Rock reflected in the water. Dennis's guests would take the elevator up to his space, where his personal assistant, Harvey, would greet them. The private elevator opened into a foyer with a wall of glass at the end that allowed guests to enjoy the view. On the right side of the room was his bedroom suite, on the left, his game room with a pool table and a bar, game tables, and a giant fireplace at the end. The kitchen and dining area adjoined the game room. Over the mantel, hung the piece of art he'd just bought for twenty-five thousand.

Harvey or one of his relatives had worked for the Moon family for generations. Even though his guests were trusted, they would be required to leave cellphones and weapons with Harvey. That was a nearly unbreakable rule. When the elevator opened and Brenda, Carol Ann, and Isabelle walked in, Harvey handed them the basket where they deposited their purses and other things they were carrying. If Brenda had been alone, it would have been different. Carol Ann was the wild card. Moon knew her history and that made him careful of her.

"What is going on with this mysterious summoning?" Brenda said as she hugged Dennis and then gasped. "Oh my god! My god!" She walked toward the painting titled *Halloween Prank*. "Where did this come from?"

Isabelle said, "It looks sort of like Brenda's hanging man sketch on steroids."

Carol Ann asked, "Did you have it painted or is this a weird coincidence?"

Dennis Moon said, "All in good time, ladies. Come on in, have cocktails, some excellent vittles, and I'll explain."

All three of them lined up in front of *Halloween Prank* and stared at it, making their observations and comments.

"Sit. I'm going to tell you girls a story, and I don't want one peep until I finish. There will be questions, I know, just let me tell it and then I will answer them all." *Maybe,* he said to himself. *But I doubt it.* "All I ask is that what I am going to tell stays in this room. Do we agree?" They shook heads yes.

"It was the beginning of spring, right at the time Max found out he had bladder cancer, and we were on the annual Walker fishing trip. Max brought up Warren Mitchell and how he would never be punished for what he did.

"Max worried he wouldn't get over the cancer and he was determined to get justice for you, Isabelle. You were working so hard to get it legally and getting nowhere. That's how it started, and I wanted retribution for myself and Bren.

"We talked more about it later, thinking of one scheme and then another. I thought of Bren's drawings and showed Max the dangling man sketch. We set out to make it happen on Halloween. Max thought then it would be his last Halloween and he was probably right.

"BigRock had the state contract on the Cantrell Road job and Max scheduled it to start in September to create a diversion near Delphi Pond. Folks would get used to the noise, the equipment, the starts and stops on the highway. I would see to it that Warren was delivered to our associates who would place him in the pond. We had a watcher in place to make sure he didn't drown.

"We thought our Halloween prank deserved an audience and we wanted the three of you to see it, but it was way too risky to tell you our plan. Best to keep you in the dark in case something went wrong, like it did.

"I asked Laurel for help here. She put forth the idea of a cleansing to help you girls get over the bad feelings caused by Warren's stealing from you. She assured me you would feel the vibe of what was happening at the pond even if you didn't witness it in person. When you saw the video, the vibe you'd felt during your ceremony would come into play and complete the healing process plus provide us with the audience we thought our prank deserved." He didn't mention Laurel Moon's role as Jana McKeller.

"Everything was going perfectly until the Blue girl showed up right before we were going to release Warren. Things got tricky. We knew Ron Cole's habit of patrolling the pond, we had studied his habits, but he usually did this before midnight. He was another surprise." Cole was the watcher, but Moon was not going to reveal that fact either.

"Our biggest surprise was when someone shot Warren." He looked at Carol Ann. He paused. "Lucky for us, Cole is the kind of man who avoids the law so he called his friend Bill Brass. None of that was planned. Luck often plays a part in a good outcome.

"After Cole hung the flashing light on Warren, my man swam out and released the valve that filled Warren's life jacket with air." Another lie they wouldn't figure out. Cole put the light around Warren's neck to give him an excuse to get near Mitchell so he could activate the vest.

"Tomorrow you will learn, as will all of Little Rock, that Warren Mitchell hired a thrill company to punish him for his failure to protect his clients from Stanford. He will say he realizes this was a sick idea and is seeking help. Or something like that. His lawyer is working it out with Chief Knight."

Just another lie to tie up the ends. Mitchell agreed to tell Brass that story for fear of what would happen to him and his family if he didn't. Brass, for his own reasons, decided to buy it.

"Bill Brass and his partner were determined to lay this at the feet of Isabelle. That worried Max, and he got sick before we could put plan B in place, but now it is in place. I told Max that Isabelle was safe so that he could rest easy.

"The painting *Halloween Prank* was going to be a gift to Max from me, a reminder of how much fun we had planning and playing the prank. Now it is a reminder to me of what I have lost with his imminent passing."

Dennis held up his glass. "To *Halloween Prank*. Revenge is best enjoyed when the revenger witnesses the full effect. Right, ladies?"

"Right," they said in unison.

"Hon, I want to know why you didn't tell us, or at least me, before now. We could have helped," Brenda said.

That's exactly what he and Max had wanted to avoid. Dennis waited a few beats before he answered.

Carol Ann noticed a slight edge in Brenda's tone and she wondered if Dennis heard it too.

"Well, Bren, if we'd told you girls then you'd be a party to it; when Brass questioned ya'll, your secret would show in your eyes. Not knowing saved you.

Secrets make you weak and vulnerable. Detectives look for what people don't want them to know."

"Brass was about to arrest me based on Dan having a gun that was the same size as the casing," Isabelle said. "Was I in real danger or not?"

"We have to look at the final outcome. The case is over and our prank successful due to our plan B. That is the important point. The casing was not enough for Brass to arrest you; he wanted you to think that, hoping to break you down. If Brass had charged you with kidnapping, it would have been dropped for lack of evidence. There's no reason to go there, it didn't happen."

Brenda, with strong emotion in her voice, said, "You're telling us that you and Max concocted a plan B that would solve any problem that came along? What if it hadn't? Then what? Would Max have taken the blame to save Isabelle, or the rest of us, or you? Or would you have sacrificed yourself, Dennis?"

Brenda stood with her left hand holding her drink, the index finger of the right pointed in his direction, and stared down at Dennis. He had never heard that tone of voice or experienced physical aggression from her. "You and Max put us in danger without our permission. It was all about ego."

Dennis didn't like what he was seeing and hearing. Brenda sounded bitchy and that reminded him of his first and second wives. Moon figured she was mad at not being included in the prank—not a good sign. It implied she felt she had a claim on him, felt entitled to know his business, and to Dennis that was a warning. It showed him what she needed. Equality, he supposed. It didn't matter. The feeling coming off her warned him to watch out. He wasn't quite sure of what but it didn't matter. The subconscious picks up on all kinds of hidden clues, and he was the type of man to listen to his inner self.

Dennis thought about telling Brenda what she wanted to hear, "I would throw myself on the fire for you, babe." Instead, he said, "Brenda, failure was not a possibility. Why go there? Max and I, we play to win, and we planned a winning strategy. That's what counts. Case closed. The only thing Max has ever failed at in his life was beating this cancer."

"Is that what counts?" Taking one step closer to him. "Truth is, you two are so selfish you never considered the impact on us if it didn't work out."

Dennis Moon rose from his chair. He didn't want an angry woman with a drink in her hand standing over him. His radar was zinging, danger. He'd made a mistake. He'd broken one of his rules—never brag—that was what he was doing by telling the story of the Halloween prank. "The problem was success-fully solved, Brenda."

"Dennis, how can you be so sure?"

Carol Ann found the whole scenario to her liking. She was glad someone besides her felt left out. After tonight, Brenda would be on her own again, with-out backup, she just didn't know it yet. For men like Dennis Moon, Brenda's actions were a deal-breaker. She wasn't his type. *If anything,* Carol Ann thought, *I am, but he isn't good-looking enough for me.*

Dennis wanted to slap Brenda across the face, tell her to shut up, quit being stupid, but he controlled his reaction. The thought crossed his mind that she might go to Brass herself. Dennis put his I-am-so-sorry-for-being-thoughtless look on his face. He took her hands in his. "Babe, you're right. I was thought-less." His mind worked to defuse the situation.

Dennis continued, "Max had a vision he was going to die sooner rather than later. We planned for his premonition. Understand this, if Max had gone to the police and taken the blame, that could give Carley Walker a reason to claim he was incompetent when he made his trust. She could also question his competency when he gave Isabelle his health care proxy. That would have prevented Isabelle from carrying out Max's health care directive. We would not have carried out the project, if we were not certain we had all possibilities covered."

Carol Ann saw Brenda open her mouth to say something. She spoke out before her friend had a chance to do any more damage. Carol Ann knew, it was over for Dennis. In an emotional tone, she said, "If Jim Bud were alive, would you have included him in on this?"

She felt like the fifth wheel. "Max wanted to do this for Isabelle, and you wanted to do it for Brenda, but there was no one thinking about doing it for me." She paused feeling herself start to choke up. "I'm glad I shot him. Even though it caused trouble."

"Are you telling me you knew it was Warren?" Dennis asked, as he and Brenda sat down on the love seat together. He pretended to listen to Carol Ann, instead he was thinking about how he was going to delete Brenda Katz from his life without drama.

"I didn't," Carol Anne said. "I had a feeling it was Warren. Now, I realize it was Jim Bud speaking to me from the other side. His way of getting in on it so someone would be taking up for me. I see now, I wasn't alone. Jim Bud was there in spirit for me."

Dennis wasn't going to go on that journey with her. She would have to go to see Laurel Moon for that.

In her heart, Isabelle had known all along Max had something to do with the Halloween prank. She could see it in his eyes the night he came by after the detectives had interviewed her.

Max never turned the other cheek. She was glad he witnessed the full effect of his revenge. Isabelle raised her glass to her dying son, the creative thinker, the prankster who loved Halloween, his favorite holiday.

About the Author

A graduate of the University of Arkansas at Little Rock, H. K. Finley holds a master's degree in public history. She has written the history of St. Vincent Hospital and is the author of *The Worthy Cause*, the first in the Delphi Pond series. She lives in Maui.

www.ingramcontent.com/pod-product-compliance
Lightning Source LLC
Chambersburg PA
CBHW060139130626
46556CB00006B/2416